ELENA ROSEWOOD

A Lady's Secret Indulgence

Regency Erotic Romance

First edition

This book was professionally typeset on Reedsy.
Find out more at reedsy.com

Contents

Prologue

Lady Beatrice Harrington could not endure another moment of Lady Caroline Blackwood's tinkling laughter or the vapid conversation floating through the drawing room of Thornfield Estate. Under the guise of a mild headache, she excused herself from the gathering, ignoring her mother's disapproving glance. The first evening of Mrs. Thornfield's infamous summer house party had barely begun, and already Beatrice longed for solitude.

Three more weeks of this torture, she thought, smoothing down the silk of her dove-gray evening gown as she slipped into the corridor. The modestly cut bodice with its high neckline and long sleeves reflected her usual reserved style, though she had allowed her lady's maid to add a slightly more fashionable trim of silver embroidery along the empire waistline.

Rather than retreating to her bedchamber, Beatrice followed the familiar path to the library. Mrs. Eleanor Thornfield, a distant cousin of her mother's, was known for her impressive collection of books—the primary reason Beatrice had agreed to attend the seasonal gathering in the first place.

The library doors yielded with a satisfying creak. Inside, the vast room was dimly lit by a dying fire and a few strategically placed candelabras. Shelves towered to the ceiling, filled with leather-bound volumes that made Beatrice's heart quicken in a way no gentleman ever had. The scent of paper, leather, and beeswax enveloped her as she closed the door behind her.

"Finally," she whispered, unpinning the tight chignon at the base of her neck. Her chestnut hair tumbled down past her shoulders, and she massaged her scalp in relief. No one would disturb her here—the other guests were far too occupied with their flirtations and gossip to seek out dusty tomes.

Beatrice wandered the shelves, trailing her fingertips along the spines. Near the back corner, a shelf of philosophy caught her attention. As she pulled out a volume of Rousseau, something clattered to the floor behind the books. Kneeling, her full skirts pooling around her on the Persian carpet, she discovered a small panel in the wall had come loose.

"How curious," she murmured, her voice barely audible even in the silent room.

Reaching into the dark cavity, her fingers closed around something cool and leather-bound. She withdrew a slim journal, unmarked except for the fine quality of its binding. Beatrice glanced over her shoulder—the library remained empty—before carrying her discovery to a wingback chair positioned close to a candelabra.

The diary's pages were filled with an elegant masculine script. There was no name, no identifying information on the first page—only a date from the previous year and the beginning of an entry:

May 15, 1815

Prologue

I have decided to record my most private thoughts and experiences in these pages, as they are fit for no one's eyes but my own. Society demands a mask of propriety that suffocates the soul, yet beneath that mask burns desires that would shock the ton into apoplexy...

Beatrice's cheeks warmed at the intimate nature of the writing, but something compelled her to continue. She turned the page, and her breath caught in her throat.

Her body was a revelation beneath the restrictive layers of society's armor. As I slowly untied the laces of her corset, she gasped with each loosening, her breasts straining against the thin chemise beneath. When the stiff garment finally gave way, I slid it from her body, revealing the perfect curves convention forces her to flatten and restrain.

"Please," she whispered, her voice rough with desire as I pressed her against the bookshelf. Leather-bound volumes surrounded us as I lifted her thighs to wrap around my waist. The feel of her silk stockings against my hands as I pushed her skirts upward nearly undid me completely...

The entry continued with explicit detail—the sensation of bare skin against book bindings, the taste of a woman's arousal, the precise movements that brought her to ecstasy against the library shelves. Beatrice's hand trembled as she read, her own body responding with unfamiliar heat pooling low in her abdomen.

She slammed the book closed, her breathing uneven.

This is utterly improper, she thought, even as her fingers itched to open the journal again. *I should return it immediately.*

But to whom? The author remained anonymous, though the handwriting suggested education and breeding. Her mind immediately conjured the image of Lord James Ashworth, the Earl of Westmoreland. His reputation as a rake preceded him, though he maintained an air of cold aloofness in society. She had observed him earlier that evening, standing apart from the crowd, his sharp blue eyes surveying the room with thinly veiled disdain.

Beatrice opened the journal again, this time flipping through until another passage caught her eye:

What these simpering debutantes fail to understand is that true passion requires mind as well as body. I find myself increasingly bored with empty physical gratification. I yearn for a woman who challenges me intellectually even as she surrenders physically—someone whose clever words arouse me as much as her form.

"Lord Ashworth," she whispered to herself. The sentiment matched what little she knew of the man—his rumored intelligence, his obvious disinterest in the usual societal games. The handwriting, elegant yet masculine, seemed to fit him as well.

The clock on the mantel chimed ten, startling Beatrice from her thoughts. She should return to her chambers before her absence became conspicuous. Instead of replacing the journal, however, she found herself slipping it into the hidden pocket her maid had sewn into her gown.

Just for tonight, she promised herself. *I'll return it tomorrow after I've... confirmed my suspicions about its owner.*

As she re-pinned her hair and straightened her gown, Beatrice couldn't ignore the unfamiliar sensation tingling through her body—curiosity mingled with something darker and more primal. For the first time in her three seasons on the marriage market, she found herself eager for the social events to come—if only to observe Lord Ashworth with new eyes.

She blew out the candle beside her chair and slipped from the library, the weight of the journal against her thigh a thrilling secret. Behind her, the loose panel in the wall remained slightly ajar, waiting for its next visitor.

Chapter 1

The morning room at Thornfield Estate bustled with activity as ladies congregated over tea and gentlemen discussed plans for the day's shooting party. Beatrice, who had barely slept after reading half the journal into the early hours, sat by the window attempting to focus on her embroidery while stealing glances at Lord Ashworth.

He cut an imposing figure in his perfectly tailored morning coat of deep navy, which emphasized the breadth of his shoulders. His cravat was tied with mathematical precision, and his buff-colored breeches clung to powerful thighs before disappearing into gleaming Hessian boots. Unlike many gentlemen who seemed uncomfortable in their formal attire, Lord Ashworth wore his clothing with the easy confidence of a man who knew his own worth.

Could those elegant hands that now hold a teacup be the same ones that wrote such scandalous prose? Beatrice wondered, her needle pausing mid-stitch.

As if sensing her scrutiny, Lord Ashworth's penetrating blue gaze suddenly met hers across the room. Beatrice immediately dropped her eyes to her embroidery, mortified at being caught staring. When she dared to look up again moments later, she found him still watching her, one eyebrow slightly raised in what might have been curiosity or amusement.

"Lady Beatrice," came the overly sweet voice of Lady Caroline Blackwood as she swept into the vacant chair beside her. "You disappeared so early last night. Were you truly indisposed, or merely bored with our company?"

Caroline's golden curls were arranged in an elaborate style that framed her heart-shaped face perfectly. Her morning dress of pale pink muslin was cut noticeably lower than was proper for daytime, revealing the swell of her generous bosom. A string of pearls drew further attention to her décolletage.

"A slight headache, nothing more," Beatrice replied politely, though she had little patience for Caroline's obvious fishing expedition.

"How fortunate you've recovered," Caroline said with false sincerity. "Lord Ashworth has suggested a riding party this afternoon. You do ride, don't you? Though I can't recall ever seeing you participate at Richmond Park during the Season."

"I ride quite well, actually," Beatrice responded, her voice cooler than intended. "My brother Thomas ensured I was properly taught."

"Splendid!" Caroline's eyes glittered with mischief. "Though I must warn you, Lord Ashworth sets a demanding pace. I've always managed to keep up with him, but it can be quite... vigorous."

The suggestive tone was not lost on Beatrice, who felt a flash of irritation at the woman's transparent double entendre. Before she could formulate a suitably cutting response, Mrs.

Thornfield approached their corner.

"Lady Beatrice, I've been meaning to ask if my library meets with your approval," the older woman said warmly. "Your mother mentioned your fondness for literature."

Beatrice flushed, thinking of what she'd discovered in that very library. "It's magnificent, Mrs. Thornfield. I've never seen such an extensive private collection."

From across the room, Lord Ashworth's deep voice suddenly joined their conversation. "You're a reader, Lady Beatrice? How unexpected."

She turned to find him standing closer than anticipated, his imposing height forcing her to tilt her chin upward to meet his gaze. Up close, she could see the flecks of darker blue in his eyes and the slight shadow of stubble along his sharp jawline.

"Because ladies ought to confine themselves to fashion plates and gossip, my lord?" she challenged, immediately regretting her sharp tone.

To her surprise, the corner of his mouth lifted in what might almost be a smile. "On the contrary. I simply meant that most young ladies of the ton claim literary interests only to appear accomplished, when in truth they've never ventured beyond Mrs. Radcliffe's gothic romances."

"And how would you categorize my literary interests, Lord Ashworth, when you know nothing of them?" Beatrice asked, her heartbeat quickening as she thought of his journal hidden in her chambers.

His eyes seemed to darken slightly. "I wouldn't presume to categorize you at all, Lady Beatrice. I find hasty classifications often miss the most... intriguing aspects of complex subjects."

The tension between them was palpable, and Beatrice found herself struggling to maintain her composure. Caroline cleared her throat pointedly.

"The riding party, Lord Ashworth? You were explaining the route you've planned."

His gaze lingered on Beatrice for a moment longer before he turned to Caroline. "Yes, I thought we might ride to the eastern ridge. The view of the valley is particularly fine."

"Will you join us, Lady Beatrice?" Mrs. Thornfield asked. "The exercise would do you good after your headache last night."

"I would be delighted," Beatrice replied, not missing the flash of annoyance that crossed Caroline's face.

"Excellent," Lord Ashworth said. "Two o'clock, then. Don't be late."

As the gathering dispersed to prepare for the day's activities, Beatrice hurried to her chambers. Her lady's maid, Frances, was laying out potential riding outfits when she entered.

"The forest green, I think," Beatrice said decisively, indicating her best riding habit. The dark green wool jacket with its military-inspired gold braiding and buttons would showcase her trim waist, while the matching skirt would drape elegantly over her legs when mounted sidesaddle.

"An excellent choice, my lady," Frances replied, clearly surprised by Beatrice's sudden interest in her appearance. "Shall I style your hair in a simple chignon beneath your hat? It would be most practical for riding."

"Yes, but perhaps with a few curls framing my face," Beatrice suggested, uncharacteristically concerned with how she would look.

As Frances helped her change from her morning dress, Beatrice's thoughts returned to the hidden diary. She had several hours before the riding party—enough time to read more and perhaps begin her own contribution.

Once alone, she retrieved the journal from its hiding place beneath her mattress and opened to where she had left off the night before. The entry described an encounter with a widow at a country house not unlike Thornfield. The explicit detail with which the author described pleasuring the woman with his mouth made Beatrice's cheeks burn and her body respond in ways she'd never experienced.

I knelt before her, slowly rolling down each silk stocking before placing my lips against her inner thigh. The sound she made when my tongue finally found her most intimate place was like music—half-shame, half-pleasure as she gripped my hair and urged me deeper...

Beatrice closed her eyes, her breathing shallow. The pressure of her corset suddenly felt constricting in a new way, pushing her breasts upward as her nipples hardened against the thin chemise beneath. Her hand drifted downward, hovering over the layers of her skirt where an insistent ache had begun to build.

This is madness, she thought, even as her fingers pressed against the fabric, seeking relief. *Ladies do not touch themselves in such a manner.*

But the vivid imagery from the journal would not leave her mind. Hesitantly at first, then with growing boldness, she allowed her hand to slip beneath her skirts. Through her drawers, she could feel the heat of her own body as she pressed her palm against the apex of her thighs.

A small gasp escaped her lips at the sensation. Never had she dared such exploration before. The combination of shame and pleasure was intoxicating as she moved her fingers in small circles, mimicking what she'd read in the journal.

Is this what it feels like to be touched by someone like Lord

Ashworth? The thought came unbidden, accompanied by an image of his strong hands replacing her own. The fantasy intensified the building tension within her.

Her breathing quickened as pressure built deep inside. She bit her lip to keep from making noise, her hips moving slightly against her hand. Just as she felt herself approaching some unknown threshold, a knock at the door made her snatch her hand away, mortified.

"Lady Beatrice?" Frances called through the door. "Your riding boots have been polished. May I bring them in?"

"One moment!" Beatrice called, her voice unnaturally high. She quickly straightened her clothing and slid the journal under a cushion before allowing her maid to enter.

Throughout the process of dressing for the riding party, Beatrice could not shake the lingering sensations her brief self-exploration had awakened. Nor could she stop thinking about the diary and its mysterious author.

As Frances fastened the last button on her riding jacket, Beatrice made a decision. After the ride, she would return to the journal—but this time, she would leave her own mark upon its pages.

Chapter 2

The riding party assembled on the sweeping gravel drive of Thornfield Estate shortly before two. Beatrice arrived precisely on time to find Lord Ashworth already mounted on a magnificent black stallion. His riding attire emphasized his athletic build—the tailored jacket hugging broad shoulders, his muscular thighs evident in tight buckskin breeches. He wore no hat, and the breeze ruffled his dark hair as he gave instructions to the grooms.

A stable hand helped Beatrice mount her assigned mare, a gentle chestnut with a white blaze. The sidesaddle positioned her so that her forest green skirt draped elegantly over the horse's flank. She adjusted her small black riding hat, conscious of the few artfully arranged curls Frances had styled around her face.

"You ride well, Lady Beatrice," Lord Ashworth commented, maneuvering his stallion alongside her mare as the party of eight began to move down the drive. "Your posture suggests actual skill rather than mere ornamental horsemanship."

Chapter 2

"My brother is a cavalry officer, my lord," she replied. "He considered it his duty to ensure I could manage more than a sedate walk around a park."

A genuine smile transformed Lord Ashworth's normally austere features. "Then perhaps you'll appreciate a more vigorous pace than these affairs usually permit. Once we reach the meadow, shall we see what these horses can do?"

The challenge in his eyes sent a thrill through Beatrice that had nothing to do with horsemanship. "I would welcome it, sir."

Lady Caroline, who had positioned herself on Lord Ashworth's other side in a striking crimson riding habit cut daringly close to her figure, pouted visibly. "James, you promised to show me the view from the ridge. I'll not have you galloping off with Lady Beatrice."

Beatrice noted the familiar use of his given name with interest. Had Caroline already established such intimacy with Lord Ashworth, or was she merely presuming upon acquaintance?

"The ridge is our destination, Caroline," he replied without looking at her. "But the journey need not be tedious for those with skill enough to make it interesting."

The party proceeded at a genteel pace until they reached a vast meadow bordered by woodland. Without warning, Lord Ashworth shot Beatrice a challenging look before spurring his stallion forward into a gallop. Without hesitation, she did the same, feeling the exhilarating rush of speed as her mare responded eagerly.

The wind whipped at her face as she leaned forward, maintaining perfect balance despite the awkward constraints of the sidesaddle. Her heart pounded with excitement as she urged her mount faster, closing the gap between herself and

Lord Ashworth. Behind them, she could hear exclamations of surprise from the rest of the party, but she paid them no mind.

For several glorious minutes, they raced across the meadow side by side, neither speaking, both reveling in the freedom of speed and skill. Beatrice felt more alive than she had in months of London drawing rooms and ballrooms. When they finally slowed their mounts at the edge of the woodland, she was laughing breathlessly, a few strands of hair having escaped their pins to frame her flushed face.

Lord Ashworth regarded her with new interest. "You ride like you have secrets, Lady Beatrice."

The comment, so unexpected and eerily perceptive, caused her laughter to fade. "What an odd thing to say, my lord."

"Is it?" His intense gaze made her feel as though he could see straight through to the journal hidden in her chamber. "People reveal themselves in how they move, in what gives them pleasure. Most ladies of your standing ride to be seen, not to feel. Yet you clearly ride for the sensation itself."

Beatrice's mouth went dry. "And what does that reveal about me, sir?"

"That there is more beneath your proper facade than you allow the world to see." His voice lowered. "I find myself curious about what else gives you pleasure, Lady Beatrice."

The arrival of the rest of the party prevented her from responding to this shockingly forward comment. Caroline looked positively murderous as she brought her horse to an abrupt halt beside them, her perfectly arranged golden curls now slightly disheveled.

"How utterly reckless," she admonished, though it was unclear whether she was more concerned about the propriety of the gallop or the private conversation she'd interrupted.

"James, you might have warned us you intended to race like schoolboys."

"My apologies, Caroline," he replied without sounding remotely sorry. "Lady Beatrice and I got carried away by the fine weather and excellent mounts."

The remainder of the ride proceeded more conventionally, though Beatrice was acutely aware of Lord Ashworth's gaze returning to her frequently. The view from the eastern ridge was indeed spectacular, with the estate visible in the distance and the river winding through the valley below.

As they paused to admire the vista, Lord Ashworth brought his horse close to Beatrice's once more. "You should visit the library again tonight," he said quietly. "Mrs. Thornfield has some excellent volumes on horsemanship that might interest you."

Before she could question this strange suggestion, he had moved away to answer a query from one of the other gentlemen. The ride back to the estate was conducted at a more sedate pace, with Beatrice pondering whether his comment had been innocent or if he somehow knew about her discovery.

* * *

That evening, after a formal dinner during which Lord Ashworth had been seated far from her, Beatrice retired to her chamber early. She dismissed Frances after changing into her nightgown and robe, claiming she wished to read before sleeping. Once alone, she retrieved the hidden journal and a small pot of ink and quill she had borrowed from the writing desk in her chamber.

For nearly an hour, she read more entries, each more explicit than the last. The writer detailed not only physical encounters but the psychology behind them—the power of making a normally controlled woman come apart with pleasure, the vulnerability of revealing one's darkest desires, the emptiness that followed meaningless trysts.

Finally, Beatrice dipped her quill in ink and, heart pounding, wrote in a small, neat hand in the margin beside a particularly evocative passage:

Your words create vivid pictures that stir unfamiliar sensations. I wonder if the reality could possibly match the artistry of your descriptions? - A Curious Reader

She blew gently on the ink until it dried, then closed the journal. Tonight, she would return it to its hiding place in the library. If Lord Ashworth was indeed the author, she wanted to observe his reaction upon discovering her note.

Donning her robe over her nightgown—a simple white cotton garment with a modest neckline and long sleeves—Beatrice slipped the journal into her pocket. She took a single candle and made her way silently through the darkened corridors of Thornfield Estate, grateful that the guest rooms were on a different floor from the library.

The vast room was illuminated only by moonlight filtering through the tall windows when she entered. She moved carefully toward the back corner where she'd found the journal. As she approached the philosophy section, she froze at the sound of a book being closed.

"I wondered if you might return tonight," came Lord Ashworth's deep voice from the shadows.

Beatrice nearly dropped her candle, her heart leaping into her throat. "Lord Ashworth! I—I didn't realize anyone was here."

Chapter 2

He emerged from a wingback chair positioned in the darkest corner of the room. He had removed his evening coat and cravat, his white shirt open at the collar to reveal the strong column of his throat. His dark hair was slightly disheveled, as if he'd run his hands through it repeatedly. In the dim light, his face was all planes and shadows, his expression unreadable.

"Evidently," he replied, moving closer. "Though I believe you were expecting to find this section unoccupied."

Beatrice clutched the journal tighter in her pocket. "I merely wished to return a book before retiring."

His eyes, dark in the candlelight, moved to where her hand pressed against her robe. "A book you apparently keep on your person rather than carrying openly. How interesting."

"I don't owe you explanations for my reading habits, my lord," she said, lifting her chin defiantly despite her racing pulse.

"No, you don't," he agreed, stopping barely an arm's length from her. He was close enough that she could detect the faint scent of brandy on his breath and something else—sandalwood and leather, masculine and intoxicating. "However, I find myself intensely curious about what literary work would bring a properly raised young lady to the library in her nightclothes."

Beatrice became acutely aware of her state of undress—the thin cotton nightgown beneath her silk robe, her hair hanging loose past her shoulders, her feet in delicate slippers rather than proper shoes. The impropriety of their situation suddenly struck her full force.

"I should return to my room," she said, taking a step backward.

"Without returning your book?" he challenged softly. "That seems to defeat the purpose of your midnight excursion, Lady Beatrice."

She swallowed hard, caught in her own deception. "How did you know I would come tonight?"

His lips curved in a slight smile. "I didn't know with certainty. But after our conversation this afternoon, I suspected you might have discovered something in this library worth revisiting. Something that perhaps revealed secrets... or inspired you to explore your own."

The implication in his words was unmistakable. Beatrice felt heat rising to her cheeks, grateful for the dim light that concealed her blush.

"You're being deliberately cryptic, my lord," she said, striving to keep her voice steady.

"As are you, my lady," he countered. His gaze dropped to her pocket once more. "What is it you're hiding?"

A moment of tense silence stretched between them. Finally, Beatrice made a decision. She withdrew the journal from her pocket and held it up.

"I believe this might belong to you," she said quietly.

Instead of the shock or anger she expected, Lord Ashworth's expression revealed only intense interest. He made no move to take the journal.

"And if it did?" he asked, his voice dropping lower. "What would you think of the man who wrote those pages?"

"I would think," Beatrice said carefully, "that he reveals more truth on paper than he ever does in society. That beneath his cold exterior lies a passionate nature. That he understands the difference between mere physical release and true connection."

Lord Ashworth moved closer still, close enough that she could feel the heat radiating from his body. "And did those truths frighten you, Lady Beatrice? Or did they awaken something within you?"

The directness of his question stole her breath. This conversation had veered far beyond the boundaries of propriety, yet she could not bring herself to retreat.

"Both," she admitted, her voice barely above a whisper.

His hand rose slowly to brush a strand of hair from her face, the brief contact sending a shock through her system. "Did you read all of it?"

"Most," she confessed. "And I… I left something of myself within its pages."

His eyebrows rose slightly. "Did you indeed? Then I shall look forward to discovering your contribution."

With unexpected gentleness, he took the journal from her trembling fingers. Their hands brushed in the exchange, and Beatrice felt the contact like a current through her body.

"You should return to your chamber, Lady Beatrice," he said softly. "Before someone discovers us and draws conclusions that would damage your reputation beyond repair."

"And what conclusions would you draw, my lord?" she dared to ask.

His gaze traveled slowly from her eyes to her lips, then lower to where her robe parted slightly at the neck, revealing the edge of her nightgown. "That curiosity is a powerful and dangerous force when combined with attraction."

The word 'attraction' hung in the air between them. Beatrice found herself unable to move, caught in the intensity of his gaze.

"Good night, Lady Beatrice," he finally said, stepping back. "I suspect we both have much to reflect upon before morning."

"Good night, Lord Ashworth," she managed, gathering her composure enough to turn and walk steadily to the door, though her legs felt unsteady beneath her.

As she slipped back to her chamber, her mind raced with questions. Had she confirmed he was the author, or had she revealed her own improper behavior to an innocent party? What would he think of her margin note? And most disturbing of all—why did the dangerous tension between them excite rather than terrify her?

That night, sleep eluded Beatrice entirely as she relived their encounter in the library, imagining alternative endings where he closed the distance between them completely.

Chapter 3

Morning found Beatrice bleary-eyed but resolute. She instructed Frances to dress her in her most becoming day dress—a light blue muslin with delicate white embroidery along the modest neckline and short puffed sleeves. The empire waistline accentuated her slim figure, while the color brought out the amber flecks in her hazel eyes.

"You seem particularly concerned with your appearance today, my lady," Frances commented as she arranged Beatrice's chestnut hair in a more elaborate style than usual, with artful curls framing her face. "Might there be a gentleman who has caught your attention?"

"Nonsense," Beatrice replied too quickly. "I merely wish to do justice to Mrs. Thornfield's hospitality."

The knowing look in her maid's eyes suggested she wasn't fooled, but Frances merely said, "Of course, my lady. The blue ribbon, I think, to match your eyes."

As she descended to breakfast, Beatrice's stomach fluttered with nervousness. How would Lord Ashworth regard her in the light of day after their clandestine encounter? Had he read her note? Was he disgusted by her boldness or intrigued?

The breakfast room was already half-full when she entered. Lord Ashworth stood by the window in conversation with her brother, Thomas, who had arrived late the previous night. They made an interesting contrast—Thomas fair-haired and open-faced in his regimental red coat, Lord Ashworth dark and intense in a bottle-green morning coat and fawn breeches.

Both men turned at her entrance. Thomas's face lit up with brotherly affection, while Lord Ashworth's expression remained carefully neutral, though his eyes sharpened with interest as they swept over her appearance.

"Bea!" Thomas exclaimed, crossing to kiss her cheek. "You look well. Country air agrees with you."

"As does military life with you," she replied warmly. "When did you arrive?"

"Near midnight. I was sorry to miss dinner, but my commanding officer kept me longer than expected." He lowered his voice. "I've been hearing interesting things about your Lord Ashworth this morning."

"He is not *my* Lord Ashworth," she hissed, conscious of the man in question watching their exchange.

Thomas's eyebrows rose in amusement. "The lady doth protest too much, methinks. He's actually requested that you join him for a ride this morning. Just the two of you. Rather forward of him, wouldn't you say?"

Beatrice's heart skipped. "What did you tell him?"

"That as your brother and temporary guardian while Father is abroad, I would be delighted to accompany you both." Thomas grinned at her obvious dismay. "Come now, Bea. You can't seriously think I'd allow you to ride out alone with the most notorious rake in three counties?"

"His reputation is exaggerated," she found herself saying defensively.

"Is it? And how would you know that after less than two days' acquaintance?" Thomas regarded her curiously. "Unless there's something you're not telling me."

Before she could formulate a response, Lord Ashworth himself approached them. Up close, Beatrice could see the subtle signs of a restless night in the faint shadows beneath his eyes—eyes that regarded her with new awareness.

"Lady Beatrice," he said with a formal bow. "Your brother has kindly agreed to join us for a morning ride, if you're amenable."

"I would be delighted, my lord," she replied, proud of how steady her voice sounded despite the riot of emotions his presence provoked.

"Excellent. Shall we say half past ten? The morning mist should have cleared by then." His gaze held hers a moment longer than was strictly proper. "I believe you'll find today's excursion most... illuminating."

The way he emphasized the last word made her wonder if he had indeed read her annotation. The thought sent a thrill of anticipation through her body.

* * *

The morning ride began in silence as the three riders set out from Thornfield Estate. Thomas, ever the soldier, took point and led them along a different path than yesterday's excursion—this one winding through woodland toward what Lord Ashworth described as an ancient Roman ruin.

"I wasn't aware Thornfield Estate contained historical sites,"

Beatrice commented as they rode side by side, Thomas several yards ahead.

"Most aren't," Lord Ashworth replied. "The ruins aren't on any formal maps. Local legend claims they were once a temple to Diana, though in truth they're likely the remains of a Roman bath complex."

"How do you know of them, then?"

A smile played at the corners of his mouth. "I make it my business to discover hidden treasures wherever I travel, Lady Beatrice. As, it seems, do you."

The reference to her discovery of the journal was unmistakable. She glanced toward her brother to ensure he remained out of earshot before responding.

"And did you discover anything of interest in your reading last night, my lord?" she asked, her heart pounding.

"Indeed," he murmured, his voice dropping to ensure their privacy. "A most unexpected annotation from a 'Curious Reader.' Imagine my surprise to find someone had not only discovered my private journal but had the audacity to contribute to it."

So he had confirmed it—the journal was his. Beatrice felt simultaneously vindicated and mortified.

"Perhaps the reader was moved by the power of the author's words," she suggested, keeping her eyes fixed ahead. "Perhaps she found herself experiencing sensations she'd never encountered in society's dry tomes or vapid conversations."

"She?" Lord Ashworth raised an eyebrow. "You seem quite certain of the reader's gender."

Beatrice's cheeks warmed. "A reasonable assumption, given the content."

"Is it?" He leaned slightly closer, though still maintaining a proper distance. "I find many assumptions about what men and women desire to be woefully inaccurate. Society prescribes such narrow channels for passion, particularly for ladies of quality."

"While men are free to explore theirs?" she challenged.

"Hardly," he scoffed. "Men are equally confined, just in different cages. We're expected to seek physical release without emotion, to separate body from soul as if such division were possible. To be both experienced libertines and faithful husbands. The contradictions are maddening."

Beatrice had never heard a gentleman speak so frankly about such matters. The honesty in his voice matched what she'd read in his journal—a man struggling against society's expectations while longing for something more authentic.

"Is that why you write?" she asked softly. "To reconcile those contradictions?"

His penetrating gaze returned to her face. "Perhaps. Or perhaps to preserve experiences that matter in a world determined to render everything meaningless. Why do you read, Lady Beatrice?"

"To discover truths I cannot learn elsewhere," she admitted. "To experience lives beyond the narrow confines of my own."

"And did my journal provide such... experiences?" The suggestive undertone made her breath catch.

"It was educational," she managed, unable to confess how his words had affected her physically.

Lord Ashworth's low chuckle sent heat spiraling through her. "Educational. What a carefully chosen word. I wonder if your contribution to my journal was equally... educational."

Before she could respond, Thomas called back to them. "We're nearly there! The path narrows ahead—we'll need to go single file."

The conversation necessarily ended as they navigated the narrower trail. After another ten minutes, they emerged into a small clearing containing the stone ruins of what had indeed once been a substantial Roman structure. Partial walls and columns created the suggestion of rooms, though the roof had long since disappeared. Nature had reclaimed much of the site, with ivy climbing the remaining stonework and wildflowers growing between flagstones.

"It's beautiful," Beatrice breathed as they dismounted. Thomas took charge of the horses, tethering them to a nearby tree where they could graze.

"I'll scout the perimeter," Thomas announced. "Make sure there are no unexpected hazards before we explore further." He strode off, his military training evident in his purposeful gait.

Left alone with Lord Ashworth, Beatrice suddenly felt the impropriety of their situation acutely. They were chaperoned only by her brother, who was temporarily out of sight. It was the closest thing to privacy they'd had since the library.

"Your brother is very protective," Lord Ashworth observed, watching Thomas disappear around a crumbling wall.

"He feels responsible for me since our mother's death," she explained. "Though I'm three and twenty and hardly in need of constant supervision."

"On the contrary," he said, moving closer. "I find you quite dangerous when left unsupervised. Breaking into private journals, writing provocative notes, visiting libraries at midnight in your nightclothes..."

Despite the teasing tone, there was unmistakable heat in his gaze as it traveled from her face down to where her riding habit hugged her figure.

"You make me sound like a character from one of Mrs. Radcliffe's gothic novels," she said, flustered by his attention.

"No, Lady Beatrice," he said softly. "You're far more interesting than any fictional heroine. Fiction follows rules. You, I suspect, are willing to break them."

"You barely know me," she protested.

"I know enough," he countered. "I know you ride with passion rather than propriety. I know you read forbidden things and respond to them. I know you're intelligent enough to recognize me as the journal's author. And I know that instead of being properly scandalized, you're intrigued."

Beatrice could not deny the truth of his assessment. Nor could she ignore how his proximity affected her—the way her pulse quickened and her skin seemed to heighten in sensitivity.

"What did you think of my response?" she asked, changing tack. "To your journal entry."

A slow smile spread across his face. "I found it promisingly bold, yet frustratingly vague. It left me wondering just what 'unfamiliar sensations' my words had stirred in you."

The directness of his question made her breath catch. "That's hardly a proper inquiry, my lord."

"We're well beyond propriety, I think." His voice lowered. "Did you touch yourself while reading my words, Lady Beatrice? Did you explore those unfamiliar sensations?"

Her face flamed at his scandalous query. "Lord Ashworth!"

"James," he corrected quietly. "If we're to exchange intimate confidences, you might as well use my given name."

"We are not exchanging intimate confidences," she insisted, though her body betrayed her with a shiver of anticipation.

"Aren't we?" He moved closer still, close enough that she

could see the varying shades of blue in his eyes. "Then allow me to begin. After reading your note, I lay awake imagining your reaction to my words. I pictured you in your bed, your proper nightgown pushed up as your fingers explored places no gentleman has touched. I wondered if you gasped, if you bit your lip to stay silent, if you found release or if you stopped yourself out of ingrained propriety."

Beatrice felt dizzy at his explicit words, spoken in that cultured voice that somehow made them even more arousing. The accuracy of his imagination was too close to what had actually occurred in her chamber.

"You should not say such things," she whispered, yet made no move to step away.

"Perhaps not," he agreed. "But propriety is a poor substitute for honesty between two people who recognize something in each other that society would prefer to suppress."

"And what do you recognize in me?" she asked, her heart hammering.

His hand rose to hover near her cheek, not quite touching. "A woman of intellect and passion beneath a carefully constructed facade. Someone who, like me, tires of meaningless social performances and craves authentic connection."

The sound of boots on stone made them step apart quickly. Thomas reappeared around the corner, his expression suspicious as he noted their proximity.

"The ruins extend farther than I expected," he announced. "There's an intact chamber with remarkable frescos just beyond that archway. You should see them before we leave."

Throughout the remainder of their exploration, Beatrice could barely focus on the archaeological wonders Thomas pointed out. Her mind kept returning to Lord Ashworth's—

James's—words and the intensity in his eyes as he'd spoken them. The realization that he had thought of her in such intimate circumstances sent waves of heat through her body.

As they rode back to Thornfield Estate, she found herself wondering whether she would have the courage to write in his journal again—and what she might confess if she did.

* * *

That evening, the house party gathered for a musical performance in the grand salon. Several young ladies had been prevailed upon to display their accomplishments at the pianoforte, including Caroline Blackwood, who performed a complicated piece with technical precision but little feeling.

Beatrice sat with her brother, conscious of Lord Ashworth's presence on the opposite side of the room. Though he appeared to be listening to the music, she noticed his gaze frequently straying in her direction. Each time their eyes met, her pulse quickened and heat rose to her cheeks.

"You're being rather obvious, Bea," Thomas murmured beside her. "Half the room has noticed your interest in Ashworth."

"I'm merely being polite," she whispered back.

"Polite doesn't involve extended eye contact and blushing," he countered. "I know you fancy yourself in love with his mind or some such nonsense—Mother always said you read too many romances—but his reputation with women is concerning."

"You don't know him," she said defensively.

"Neither do you, after two days' acquaintance." Thomas's expression softened. "I just don't want to see you hurt. Men like Ashworth view conquest as sport, not prelude to matrimony."

If only you knew the depth of his thoughts in that journal, she wanted to say. Instead, she squeezed her brother's hand. "I appreciate your concern, but I assure you, I'm not some naive debutante to be swept away by a handsome face."

As the evening progressed, Mrs. Thornfield approached where Beatrice sat. "My dear, would you favor us with a piece? I'm told you play quite beautifully."

Beatrice hesitated. She enjoyed music but had never considered her playing exceptional. "I fear I would disappoint after such accomplished performances."

"Nonsense," Mrs. Thornfield insisted. "Sometimes feeling matters more than technical perfection. Please, I would consider it a personal favor."

Unable to refuse her hostess, Beatrice made her way to the pianoforte. Settling her skirts around her on the bench, she took a moment to compose herself before beginning a Beethoven sonata she had long favored—one that required more emotional interpretation than showy technique.

As she played, she became lost in the music, her fingers finding the keys without conscious thought. The piece had always moved her with its shifts between melancholy and hope, and she poured her confused emotions into the performance.

When she finished, the applause seemed genuinely appreciative rather than merely polite. She rose from the bench, her gaze inevitably finding Lord Ashworth's. The intensity of his expression—admiration mingled with something darker and more primal—made her breath catch.

"Beautifully done, Lady Beatrice," Mrs. Thornfield said warmly. "Such sensitivity in your interpretation."

"Indeed," came Lord Ashworth's voice as he approached. "You play with surprising passion, Lady Beatrice."

"Thank you, my lord," she replied, conscious of the double

meaning in his words.

"I wonder if you might assist me," he continued. "I was just telling Mrs. Thornfield that I recall seeing a volume of Beethoven's works in the library that contains some lesser-known pieces. Perhaps you might help me locate it? I'm sure the company would appreciate hearing something novel."

The transparent excuse to get her alone might have been amusing if it weren't so effective. Mrs. Thornfield's knowing smile suggested she wasn't fooled but chose to be accommodating.

"What an excellent idea," their hostess said. "The library can be quite confusing for those unfamiliar with my organizational system."

Beatrice glanced at her brother, who frowned in disapproval. "Perhaps Thomas should accompany us. He has an excellent memory for music."

"Nonsense," Mrs. Thornfield interjected before Thomas could agree. "Your brother promised to tell me more about his regiment's recent activities in France. We'll join you shortly."

With no graceful way to refuse, Beatrice found herself walking beside Lord Ashworth through the corridors toward the library. The moment they were out of earshot of the salon, he spoke in a low voice.

"I've left a response to your note," he said without preamble. "In the journal."

Her pulse quickened. "You wrote back to me?"

"Did you think I wouldn't?" He glanced down at her, his eyes reflecting the lamplight from the corridor sconces. "Your comment deserved a proper reply."

They reached the library, which was blessedly empty. Lord Ashworth closed the door behind them, leaving it slightly ajar for propriety's sake, though anyone passing would assume they were indeed searching for sheet music.

He crossed directly to the philosophy section and reached behind the loose panel, withdrawing the familiar leather-bound journal. "Here," he said, offering it to her. "Page forty-three."

With trembling fingers, Beatrice accepted the journal and opened it to the indicated page. There, beside her own neat annotation, was a new entry in his elegant script:

My Curious Reader - The reality would surpass any description, for words cannot fully capture the heat of skin against skin, the taste of desire, or the sound of pleasure unrestrained. I find myself wondering what other curiosities lurk behind your proper facade, and how exquisite it would be to explore them together. - The Author

Heat bloomed in her core at his words. When she looked up, she found him watching her reaction with undisguised interest.

"That's rather presumptuous," she managed, though her voice lacked conviction.

"Is it?" he asked softly. "Or merely honest? Would you prefer polite fiction to raw truth, Beatrice?"

The use of her given name without title sent a thrill through her. It was a liberty no gentleman should take with an unmarried lady of quality, yet in this moment, social rules seemed absurdly restrictive.

"I prefer honesty," she admitted. "Though society rarely rewards it."

"Society isn't present at this moment," he pointed out, moving closer. "Just you and I and the words we've exchanged."

Beatrice clutched the journal to her chest like a shield. "What do you want from me, James?"

"Everything," he said simply. "Your thoughts, your passions, your body, your mind. But I'll settle for your continued correspondence in those pages for now."

The boldness of his declaration stunned her. No one had ever spoken to her with such raw desire, such complete disregard for convention.

"And if I refuse?" she asked, testing him.

"Then I'll respect your decision," he replied, surprising her. "Desire without consent is merely predation. I want you willing, Beatrice, not coerced."

She hadn't expected such a principled response from a man with his reputation. It aligned more with the thoughtful author of the journal than the rake of society gossip.

"I haven't decided yet," she said, neither accepting nor rejecting his proposition.

He nodded, a slight smile playing at his lips. "Fair enough. Keep the journal tonight. Write your response—whatever it may be. I'll check tomorrow."

The door to the library opened wider as Thomas entered, his expression suspicious. "Found your music yet?"

"Alas, no," Lord Ashworth replied smoothly. "Lady Beatrice suggested we try the music room instead. The volume may have been misplaced."

Thomas's gaze fell to the journal Beatrice still clutched. "What's that, then?"

"A volume of poetry I was showing Lord Ashworth," she improvised. "Wordsworth. Not quite what we were looking for."

If Thomas doubted her explanation, he didn't press the matter. "Mrs. Thornfield is asking for your return. The next young lady refuses to play until she has a larger audience."

"Of course," Beatrice said, slipping the journal into the pocket of her evening gown—thankfully one of her few dresses with such a practical feature. "We shouldn't keep them waiting."

As they returned to the salon, Lord Ashworth walked slightly ahead with Thomas, leaving Beatrice to her thoughts. The weight of the journal in her pocket felt significant, as did the decision before her. Should she continue this dangerous correspondence? What might it lead to? And was she willing to risk her reputation—and possibly her heart—to find out?

* * *

That night, alone in her chamber with the journal open before her on the bed, Beatrice faced her decision. Frances had helped her undress for the night, removing the elegant evening gown of cream silk with delicate gold embroidery, unlacing her corset with practiced efficiency, and brushing out her hair until it fell in glossy waves past her shoulders. Now, wearing only her thin cotton nightgown, she sat cross-legged on the bed examining James's response to her first tentative note.

The intimacy of this strange correspondence thrilled her. There was something powerfully erotic about communicating through written words—perhaps because it allowed her to express thoughts she could never voice aloud. The page became a safe space for honesty, for desires too scandalous to acknowledge in person.

She dipped her quill in ink and, after a moment's hesitation, began to write beneath his response:

The Author - Your confidence intrigues me, as does your unexpected principle regarding consent. I confess your words have awakened sensations I never permitted myself to explore before discovering your journal. Last night, alone in my bed, I touched myself while remembering one of your more explicit passages.

Chapter 3

The pleasure was both shocking and addictive, though I fear I stopped short of whatever culmination might have awaited. Perhaps experience is indeed the best teacher? - Still Curious

Her hand trembled as she wrote the shockingly forward admission. No properly raised lady would ever confess such a thing, yet the anonymity of the page gave her courage. Even though she knew he would recognize her handwriting, the confession felt less personal somehow when committed to paper rather than spoken aloud.

After the ink dried, she read her words again, blushing furiously at her own boldness. She nearly crossed out the passage, but something stopped her—perhaps the memory of the hunger in James's eyes when he looked at her, or the longing for authentic connection she'd read in his journal entries.

Closing the book, she slid from her bed and wrapped herself in a thin robe. The house was silent as she made her way to the library, candle in hand, to return the journal to its hiding place. She had just replaced the panel when a voice from the doorway made her freeze.

"I had a feeling you might visit tonight."

Beatrice spun around to find Caroline Blackwood watching her, a smug smile playing across her beautiful face. She wore an elaborate silk dressing gown in deep crimson that emphasized her voluptuous figure, her golden hair loose around her shoulders.

"Lady Caroline," Beatrice managed, trying to calm her racing heart. "I couldn't sleep and thought I might find something to read."

"Behind a loose panel in the wall?" Caroline arched a perfectly shaped eyebrow. "How fascinating. I wonder what Lord Ashworth would make of your midnight explorations?"

The explicit mention of James confirmed Beatrice's worst fears—Caroline had been watching them. "I don't know what you mean."

Caroline's laugh was musical but cold. "Please, spare me the innocent act. I saw you with him earlier this evening. The way you look at each other is hardly subtle." She moved closer, her silk dressing gown whispering against the carpet. "What I can't understand is why he's pursuing you when I've made my interest abundantly clear. You're hardly his usual type."

"Perhaps that's precisely why," Beatrice replied before she could stop herself.

Caroline's eyes narrowed. "Be careful, Lady Beatrice. Men like James Ashworth don't marry bookish spinsters with more intelligence than beauty. They amuse themselves with such novelties before returning to women who understand their true needs."

"Women like yourself?" Beatrice couldn't keep the edge from her voice.

"Precisely." Caroline's smile was predatory. "I know exactly what James wants because we're two of a kind. You're merely a temporary distraction—an experiment to see if a bluestocking can be corrupted in the bedchamber."

The crude assessment stung, though Beatrice tried not to show it. "You seem very concerned with my welfare, Lady Caroline. How touching."

"Not concern, my dear. Warning." Caroline moved to the door. "Enjoy your reading. I do hope it's educational."

After Caroline departed, Beatrice leaned against the bookshelf, her legs suddenly weak. The confrontation had shaken her more than she cared to admit. Was Caroline right? Was she merely a novel diversion for a man known for his numerous conquests?

The journal entries suggested otherwise—they revealed a man seeking meaning beyond physical gratification, a soul tired of empty encounters. But perhaps she was romanticizing what was merely the private musings of a practiced libertine.

No, she decided as she made her way back to her chamber. James's eyes held genuine interest when they spoke of matters beyond the physical. His respect for her consent spoke of character deeper than reputation suggested. Caroline's warning seemed born more of jealousy than insight.

Still, as she slipped back into bed, doubt crept in with the shadows. She had committed something dangerously revealing to paper, something that could not be unsaid. Tomorrow, James would read her confession and know the effect he had on her. What would happen then?

Sleep came fitfully, plagued by dreams of James finding her in the library, reading her words aloud in that deep voice, then showing her exactly what "culmination" she had denied herself.

Chapter 4

The following day brought rain, confining the house party guests to indoor pursuits. Beatrice spent the morning in the drawing room with several other ladies, pretending to focus on her embroidery while her mind continuously returned to the journal and what she had written. Had James found it yet? What would he think of her confession? The uncertainty was both torturous and thrilling.

Caroline Blackwood sat nearby, occasionally sending knowing smirks in Beatrice's direction that made her skin crawl. The encounter in the library hung between them like an unspoken threat.

Shortly before luncheon, Lord Ashworth entered the drawing room in conversation with Mrs. Thornfield. His tailored gray jacket emphasized the breadth of his shoulders, and his cravat was tied in a complex style that drew attention to the strong column of his throat. His dark hair was slightly damp from the rain, giving him a rakish appearance that caused several ladies to flutter their fans.

Chapter 4

Beatrice kept her eyes fixed on her embroidery, though she was painfully aware of his presence. When she finally risked a glance upward, she found him watching her with an intensity that sent heat rushing through her body. The slight smile playing at the corners of his mouth suggested he had indeed found and read her response.

Mrs. Thornfield followed his gaze and smiled knowingly. "Lord Ashworth has just been discussing the possibility of charades this evening, Lady Beatrice. Given the inclement weather, we thought some theatrical entertainment might lift everyone's spirits."

"An excellent suggestion," Beatrice replied, struggling to keep her voice steady under James's continued scrutiny.

"I suggested teams," he added, moving closer to where she sat. "Perhaps you might partner with me, Lady Beatrice? I understand you have quite the literary knowledge."

Caroline immediately inserted herself into the conversation. "James, you promised to partner with me. Have you forgotten our discussion at breakfast?"

His expression revealed nothing as he turned to Caroline. "Did I? My apologies, Lady Caroline. My memory must be failing me."

The subtle rejection made Caroline's beautiful face harden momentarily before she recovered her poise. "No matter. We can form teams of three. I'm sure Lady Beatrice won't mind joining us."

The prospect of spending the evening watching Caroline fawn over James was decidedly unappealing, but Beatrice could see no graceful way to refuse. "That would be lovely," she lied.

"Splendid!" Mrs. Thornfield declared. "We'll arrange everything for after dinner. Now, I believe luncheon is about to be served."

As the party began to move toward the dining room, James managed to position himself beside Beatrice. Under the cover of general conversation, he murmured, "Your contribution to our literary exchange was most... illuminating."

Her cheeks flamed at the reference to her written confession. "You found it, then."

"Indeed." His voice dropped lower. "I've left a response. One I think you'll find instructive regarding the... culmination you mentioned."

Before she could reply, Caroline appeared at his other side, threading her arm through his with a proprietorial air. "James, Mrs. Thornfield has seated us together at luncheon. Isn't that fortuitous?"

He extracted his arm with practiced politeness. "Quite. Though I believe I'm seated beside Lady Beatrice's brother, according to the place cards I glimpsed earlier."

Caroline's smile tightened. "How disappointing. Perhaps at dinner?"

"Perhaps," he replied noncommittally.

Beatrice couldn't help the small surge of satisfaction at Caroline's obvious frustration. Throughout luncheon, she found her appetite diminished by anticipation. Somewhere in the library, James had left another entry in their clandestine correspondence—one that promised to address her most intimate confession.

* * *

The afternoon dragged interminably. Rain continued to lash against the windows, and the planned charades were postponed until after dinner in favor of card games and conversation. Beatrice participated only minimally, her mind constantly straying to the library and the journal hidden within its walls.

Finally, as the hours for dressing for dinner approached, she found her opportunity to slip away. Claiming a desire to refresh herself before her maid arrived to help her dress, she made her way to the library with her heart pounding in her chest.

The vast room was empty as she had hoped. Moving quickly to the philosophy section, she located the loose panel and retrieved the journal with trembling fingers. Settling into a secluded window seat partially concealed by heavy velvet curtains, she opened to their ongoing exchange.

Beneath her shocking confession about touching herself, James had written a lengthy response in his elegant handwriting:

My Curious Reader - Your candor both moves and arouses me. There is nothing more intoxicating than a woman who acknowledges her own desires, especially one society has tried so diligently to convince that she shouldn't possess them. Your exploration honors your body's wisdom over society's foolishness.

As for the culmination you denied yourself—perhaps I might offer guidance? Imagine my hand replacing yours, fingers stroking slowly at first, gauging your response. I would watch your face as pleasure built, learning what makes your breath catch, what causes your back to arch. When I found that perfect rhythm, that precise pressure that makes you gasp, I would maintain it relentlessly until tremors began to course through your body.

The culmination you seek is called many things—la petite mort, release, climax—but no term adequately captures that exquisite moment when pleasure crests and breaks. Your body will tense, your inner muscles will contract rhythmically, and waves of sensation will wash through you with such intensity that for a moment, all thought ceases.

Tonight, try again. Picture me there with you. Don't stop when intensity builds—that threshold of almost-painful pleasure is merely the gateway. Push beyond it. Let yourself surrender. The experience is worth whatever imagined impropriety you fear.

I find myself painfully aroused imagining you in your bed, nightgown pushed up around your waist, fingers moving beneath it. Did you know a man can experience similar culmination? As I write this, I am hard with want of you, my body aching for release while thinking of your curious explorations.

Until our next exchange - The Author (who wishes he were your teacher in more than words)

Beatrice's breath came faster as she read his explicit instructions. The image he painted of himself aroused while thinking of her sent liquid heat pooling between her thighs. Never had she imagined a man—especially one of James's standing—confessing such vulnerability, such raw desire.

Without stopping to consider the impropriety, she retrieved the small pencil she kept in her pocket for noting interesting passages while reading. In the margin beside his entry, she quickly wrote:

Tonight I shall follow your guidance and report my findings. The thought of you similarly affected brings its own peculiar pleasure. I find myself wondering what you look like in such moments of abandon, when society's mask falls completely away. - Your Student

She had just closed the journal when the library door opened. Heart hammering, she peered around the edge of the curtain to see James himself entering the room. He moved with purpose toward the philosophy section, evidently intending to check whether she had found his message.

Chapter 4

Beatrice froze, unsure whether to reveal herself. Before she could decide, the door opened again, and Caroline Blackwood's voice filled the room.

"James! I've been looking everywhere for you."

Beatrice shrank back into the window seat, pulling the curtain slightly to better conceal herself. Through the small gap, she could see James turn to face Caroline with barely concealed impatience.

"Lady Caroline. Were you hoping to find a book as well?" His tone suggested he didn't believe her literary interests for a moment.

Caroline laughed, moving closer to him with deliberate sensuality. The afternoon dress she wore was cut lower than fashion dictated, showcasing her considerable assets. "Don't be coy, James. We both know why you've been frequenting the library, and it has nothing to do with reading."

He stiffened. "I'm not sure what you mean."

"Please." She stepped closer still, placing a hand on his chest. "I saw you with her last night. Lady Beatrice, of all people. I wouldn't have thought her your type, but I suppose even the most discerning gentleman occasionally craves novelty."

James removed her hand firmly. "My interactions with Lady Beatrice are none of your concern."

"Aren't they?" Caroline's voice hardened slightly. "We had an understanding in London, James. Or have you forgotten our arrangement at Lady Melbourne's ball?"

"That was a momentary diversion, nothing more," he replied coldly. "I made no promises."

Caroline's laugh held an edge. "A momentary diversion that lasted three nights, as I recall. Rather enthusiastic nights, at that."

From her hiding place, Beatrice felt her chest tighten painfully. So there had been something between them—exactly as Caroline had implied last night. The confirmation shouldn't have hurt given James's notorious reputation, yet it did.

"What do you want, Caroline?" James asked, his voice weary.

"The same thing I've always wanted." She moved closer again, pressing her body against his. "You. Without complications or expectations. Just pleasure between two people who understand each other."

To Beatrice's dismay, James didn't immediately step away. For a terrible moment, it seemed he might accept Caroline's proposition. Then he firmly disengaged himself.

"I'm not interested."

Caroline's beautiful face contorted with anger. "Because of her? That bookish spinster who probably wouldn't know what to do with a man if comprehensive instructions were provided?"

"Because I'm tired of meaningless encounters," he replied sharply. "And because you and I have never understood each other. We merely used each other—a distinction I've come to find significant."

Caroline stared at him in apparent disbelief before her expression shifted to calculation. "You think she's different? Sweet and innocent? Ask her about last night, James. Ask her what she was doing in this library after midnight. Ask her what she was hiding behind the panel in the wall."

Beatrice's blood ran cold. Caroline was deliberately trying to expose their correspondence.

James's expression revealed nothing. "I have no idea what you're talking about."

"Don't you?" Caroline smiled maliciously. "Perhaps I should

ask Lady Beatrice myself. Publicly. At dinner tonight."

"That would be ill-advised," he said, his voice dropping to a dangerous register Beatrice had never heard before. "Especially from someone with secrets of her own. Lord Blackwood might be interested to know who his wife was entertaining while he was in Scotland last season."

Caroline paled visibly. "You wouldn't dare."

"I would prefer not to," he agreed. "Just as you would prefer not to meddle in matters that don't concern you. Now, if you'll excuse me, I should dress for dinner."

After a tense moment, Caroline swept from the library, radiating fury. James remained still for several heartbeats after she departed, then ran a hand through his hair in evident frustration.

"You can come out now," he said quietly, turning toward the window seat.

Beatrice froze, mortified at being discovered. Slowly, she pushed aside the curtain and emerged from her hiding place, the journal clutched to her chest.

"How did you know I was there?" she asked, unable to meet his eyes.

"I didn't, until I saw the curtain move," he admitted. "Then I suspected."

Silence stretched between them, heavy with the implications of what they'd both overheard.

"Caroline and I—" he began.

"You don't owe me explanations," Beatrice interrupted. "Your past is your own."

"Perhaps." He moved closer, his expression serious. "But your opinion matters to me, which is novel enough to deserve acknowledgment."

She finally looked up, meeting his intense gaze. "Why? Why should my opinion matter when you have women like Caroline throwing themselves at you? Beautiful, experienced women who understand what you want?"

"Because they don't understand at all," he said quietly. "They see only what society has trained them to see—a wealthy titled gentleman with a certain reputation. They don't see me."

"And I do?" she challenged.

"You read my journal," he pointed out. "Not just the explicit passages, but the thoughts behind them. You responded not just to the physical descriptions but to the loneliness between the lines."

His perception startled her. She had indeed been drawn as much to the underlying yearning for connection as to the erotic content.

"I should go," she said, suddenly aware of their precarious situation. "My maid will be waiting to help me dress for dinner."

He nodded, making no move to stop her. "Will you come to the library tonight? After everyone has retired?"

The invitation was unmistakably improper—far beyond their written correspondence in its implications. Meeting a gentleman alone at night was utterly scandalous.

"Why?" she asked, though she already knew the answer.

"Because I want to speak with you properly, without fear of interruption or discovery. Because written words, while powerful, are poor substitutes for conversation. Because I want to see your face when I tell you how your honesty has affected me."

The naked vulnerability in his admission disarmed her completely. This was not the practiced seduction of a notorious rake but the genuine request of a man seeking connection.

"Midnight," she heard herself say. "After the charades and card games have concluded and the house is quiet."

Relief and something darker flashed across his face. "I'll be waiting."

As she slipped from the library, still clutching the journal, Beatrice wondered if she had just made the most reckless decision of her life. Meeting James alone at night went beyond impropriety into potential ruin if they were discovered. Yet the prospect filled her with anticipation rather than fear.

Chapter 5

Dinner passed in a blur of tension. Caroline seated herself strategically beside Thomas, engaged him in animated conversation that frequently referenced Beatrice in ways designed to draw his attention to his sister's behavior. James, seated at the opposite end of the table, maintained his usual composed facade, though Beatrice caught him watching her when he thought no one would notice.

She had dressed with particular care in her finest evening gown—a deep emerald silk that complemented her hazel eyes and chestnut hair. The neckline was lower than her usual style, though still modest by the standards of women like Caroline. The empire waistline emphasized her slim figure, while the short puffed sleeves showcased the graceful line of her arms.

After dinner came the promised charades. Teams were formed—Beatrice finding herself indeed grouped with James and Caroline despite the obvious tension between them. The forced proximity as they huddled to strategize was both torturous and thrilling. Each time James leaned close to whisper a suggestion, his breath against her ear sent shivers down her spine.

Their team performed admirably, with Beatrice's literary knowledge and James's surprising theatrical ability compensating for Caroline's deliberate sabotage attempts. By the end of the evening, even Caroline seemed to have temporarily set aside her vendetta in favor of competitive spirit.

As the clock approached eleven, guests began retiring to their chambers. Thomas gave Beatrice a pointed look as she claimed fatigue, clearly suspicious of her uncharacteristic eagerness for sleep. Mrs. Thornfield, ever the observant hostess, merely smiled knowingly as she bid Beatrice goodnight.

In her chamber, Frances helped her undress, carefully removing the emerald silk gown and unlacing her corset. Beatrice dismissed her maid earlier than usual, claiming a desire to read before sleeping. Once alone, she paced her room anxiously, alternating between anticipation and doubt about her midnight rendezvous.

When the mantel clock showed half past eleven, she changed from her nightgown into a simple day dress of pale blue muslin—less formal than her evening attire but more proper than receiving a gentleman in her nightclothes. She left her hair loose around her shoulders, a compromise between formality and the intimacy of the hour.

At precisely midnight, Beatrice slipped from her chamber and made her way through the darkened corridors of Thornfield Estate. Her single candle cast eerie shadows on the walls as she descended the stairs and approached the library. Outside the heavy oak doors, she paused, her heart pounding so loudly she was certain it could be heard throughout the silent house.

I can still turn back, she thought. *Return to my chamber, preserve my reputation, pretend this madness never began.*

Instead, she pushed open the door and entered.

The library was dimly lit by a small fire in the grate and several candles placed strategically around the room. James stood by the window, silhouetted against the night sky. He had removed his evening coat and cravat, leaving him in shirtsleeves and waistcoat—a state of undress that would be scandalous in daylight but seemed appropriate for this clandestine meeting.

He turned at the sound of the door, his expression shifting from tension to relief when he saw her. "You came."

"I said I would," she replied, closing the door softly behind her.

They stood several feet apart, the weight of their correspondence and the impropriety of their meeting hanging between them.

"Would you like some brandy?" he offered, gesturing to a decanter on a small table. "I took the liberty of bringing it from the study. I thought it might help with... nerves."

The thoughtfulness of the gesture touched her. "Yes, thank you."

He poured two small glasses, crossing to hand one to her. Their fingers brushed in the exchange, sending electricity through her body. The brandy burned pleasantly as she took a sip, liquid courage warming her from within.

"I found your latest note," he said after a moment. "Left while you were hiding from Caroline and me, I presume?"

She nodded, unable to forget the conversation she had overheard. "About that—"

"Caroline and I had a brief affair in London," he said directly, apparently determining honesty was the best approach. "Three nights, as she so crudely pointed out. It meant nothing beyond physical release. It ended when I recognized the emptiness of such encounters."

"You don't need to explain," Beatrice said, though she was secretly grateful for his candor.

"I believe I do." He moved to the fireplace, staring into the flames. "My reputation is largely deserved, Beatrice. I have pursued physical pleasure without emotional attachment for most of my adult life. I have used women who were equally using me. I make no excuses for that behavior."

"Then what has changed?" she asked quietly.

He turned to face her, his expression more vulnerable than she had ever seen it. "I have. Or perhaps I've merely acknowledged what was always true—that such encounters ultimately leave me feeling more isolated, not less. That genuine connection requires more than shared physical pleasure."

"And you think you might find that connection with me?" The question escaped before she could censor it.

"I think," he said carefully, "that in your written words and in our few conversations, I've glimpsed something that has eluded me in more physical relationships. Understanding. Recognition of something beyond the surface."

Beatrice's heart quickened at the sincerity in his voice. "Your journal revealed a similar depth to me. A man who thinks and feels beyond what society permits him to express."

"Society constrains us all in different ways," he agreed, moving closer. "Men are allowed physical expression but denied emotional vulnerability. Women are denied both."

"Not entirely," she countered. "We have our friends, our sisters. We're permitted emotional attachments."

"But not physical pleasure," he said softly. "Not without marriage, and even then, you're taught to endure rather than enjoy."

The boldness of his statement made her blush, yet she couldn't deny its truth. Everything she knew about marital relations came from whispered half-truths from married friends, who spoke of "wifely duty" rather than mutual pleasure.

"Your journal suggested otherwise," she said, meeting his gaze directly. "It described women experiencing pleasure as intense as any man's."

"Because it exists," he replied simply. "Despite society's determination to convince women their bodies aren't designed for enjoyment."

He was close enough now that she could see the varying shades of blue in his eyes, could detect the sandalwood scent of his shaving soap. Her body responded to his proximity with an immediacy that both thrilled and frightened her.

"Did you follow my guidance?" he asked, his voice dropping lower. "After reading my response?"

The intimate question made her breath catch. This was the moment to retreat to propriety, to deflect with a delicate subject change. Instead, honesty compelled her forward.

"Not yet," she admitted. "I planned to tonight... after our meeting."

His pupils dilated visibly at her confession. "And if I offered to show you instead? To guide you not just with words but with touch?"

The suggestion sent heat spiraling through her body. What he proposed went far beyond impropriety—it was potentially ruinous. Yet she couldn't deny the hunger that had been building since she first read his journal, a hunger that mere words could no longer satisfy.

"That would be madness," she whispered, not stepping away.

"Undoubtedly," he agreed, reaching up to brush a strand of hair from her face. Unlike in the library days ago, this time his fingers made contact, trailing lightly against her cheek. "The question is whether it's a madness worth embracing."

His touch, though slight, sent shivers across her skin. "If we were discovered..."

"We won't be," he assured her. "The house is asleep. The door is locked."

She hadn't even noticed him locking it. "My reputation—"

"Would remain intact unless you choose otherwise." His hand cupped her cheek fully now, his thumb tracing her lower lip with exquisite gentleness. "I would show you pleasure, Beatrice. Nothing more tonight. You would return to your chamber physically unchanged in any way society deems significant."

The implication was clear—he would not take her virginity, would not compromise her completely. The offer was both disappointingly limited and thrillingly possible because of those very limitations.

"And emotionally?" she challenged. "Would I remain unchanged in that regard as well?"

A smile touched his lips. "That, I cannot promise. Nor would I wish to."

The honesty of his admission decided her. Setting down her brandy glass, she stepped closer until barely a handspan separated them. "Show me," she whispered.

For a moment, he remained still, giving her the opportunity to reconsider. When she didn't retreat, he closed the remaining distance between them, his lips finding hers with surprising gentleness.

The kiss began softly—a question rather than a demand. His lips were warm and firm against hers, coaxing rather than conquering. Beatrice had been kissed before—chaste, awkward encounters with overeager suitors—but nothing had prepared her for the skill with which James approached even this seemingly simple act.

When her lips parted on a soft gasp, he deepened the kiss, his tongue tracing the seam of her mouth before slipping inside. The intimate invasion should have shocked her but instead sent liquid heat pooling between her thighs. Hesitantly, she met his tongue with her own, learning the rhythm he established.

His hands remained relatively proper, one cupping her face, the other resting lightly at her waist. It was Beatrice who grew bolder, moving closer until her body pressed against his, her hands rising to rest against the solid wall of his chest.

The contact seemed to break something in James's control. A low groan escaped him as his arm wrapped more firmly around her waist, pulling her fully against him. Through the layers of their clothing, she could feel the hard evidence of his desire pressing against her lower abdomen—shocking yet thrilling proof of his arousal.

When they finally broke apart for air, Beatrice was trembling with need she scarcely understood. "James," she whispered, her voice unrecognizable to her own ears.

"We can stop," he offered, though the strain in his voice suggested the offer cost him.

"No," she said firmly. "I want… I need…"

Unable to articulate what her body demanded, she pulled him back to her, initiating the kiss this time with newfound boldness. Her hands slid up to tangle in his hair, marveling at its silky texture between her fingers.

James responded in kind, his kisses growing more urgent, more demanding. His hands began to roam more freely—still avoiding her most intimate areas but learning the curves of her back, the sensitive skin of her neck, the delicate shells of her ears.

When his lips left hers to trail down her throat, Beatrice gasped at the new sensation. "Oh!"

"Too much?" he murmured against her skin.

"Not enough," she admitted breathlessly.

His soft chuckle vibrated against her neck as he continued his exploration, finding a particularly sensitive spot where her neck met her shoulder that made her knees weaken. His arm tightened around her waist, supporting her.

"Perhaps we should move somewhere more comfortable," he suggested, nodding toward a chaise longue positioned near the fire.

The suggestion brought reality crashing back momentarily. What was she doing? What would Thomas think—or worse, her father? The proper Lady Beatrice Harrington, engaging in wanton behavior with a notorious rake in the library of their hostess's home.

Yet as she looked into James's eyes, she saw not calculation but genuine desire mingled with concern for her comfort. This was not the practiced seduction of countless women before her but something more authentic—a shared exploration between two people who had already revealed their inner selves through written words.

"Yes," she decided, allowing him to guide her to the chaise.

He sat first, then gently pulled her down beside him. The new position allowed for greater intimacy, with their bodies partially reclining and pressed close together. His arm encircled her shoulders while his free hand cupped her face, bringing her in for another kiss.

This time, as their lips met, his hand began a slow journey downward, skimming lightly over her collarbone, then lower to hover just above her breast. He paused there, breaking the kiss to meet her eyes in silent question.

Wordlessly, Beatrice covered his hand with her own and guided it to her breast. Through the fabric of her dress, she felt his warm palm cup the modest swell, his thumb finding and circling the hardened peak of her nipple. The sensation sent sparks of pleasure shooting directly to her core.

"James," she gasped, arching into his touch.

Encouraged by her response, he continued his gentle exploration, using both hands now to caress her breasts through her clothing. Each circle of his thumbs over her sensitive nipples made her squirm with building need.

"May I?" he asked, his fingers moving to the small buttons that secured the bodice of her dress.

The request should have scandalized her. Instead, she found herself nodding eagerly, helping him with the tiny fastenings. As the bodice loosened, he eased it down over her shoulders, exposing her chemise beneath. The thin cotton was poor concealment for her aroused state, her nipples clearly visible through the fabric.

James groaned at the sight. "You're exquisite," he murmured, bending to place a kiss against the swell of her breast just above the chemise's edge.

The heat of his mouth through the thin fabric made Beatrice whimper. Emboldened by desire, she tugged the chemise lower, exposing her breasts completely to his gaze.

In the firelight, her skin glowed golden, her nipples tightened to dusky peaks. For a moment, James simply looked, his expression one of reverent admiration rather than mere lust.

Then slowly, giving her time to object, he lowered his head and took one nipple into his mouth.

The wet heat of his tongue against her sensitive flesh tore a cry from Beatrice's throat. Her hands flew to his hair, holding him to her breast as he suckled gently, then with increasing pressure. His hand found her other breast, kneading and plucking at the nipple to ensure equal attention.

The dual assault on her senses sent pulses of pleasure straight to the ache building between her thighs. She found herself shifting restlessly, seeking some relief for the growing tension.

Understanding her unspoken need, James's free hand moved to her ankle, then slowly up her calf, taking the hem of her dress with it. He paused at her knee, again seeking permission with his eyes.

"Yes," she whispered, spreading her legs slightly in invitation.

His hand continued its journey, slipping beneath her dress to caress the sensitive skin of her inner thigh just above her garter. The intimacy of the touch made her tremble.

"Remember what I wrote?" he murmured against her breast. "About guiding you to culmination?"

She nodded, unable to form coherent words as his fingers traced patterns on her thigh, moving ever higher.

"I'm going to touch you now," he said, his voice a rough caress. "If you want me to stop at any point, just say so. Do you understand?"

"Yes," she managed. "Please, James. Touch me."

His hand moved higher, finally reaching the juncture of her thighs. Through the thin fabric of her drawers, he could feel the heat and dampness of her arousal. Beatrice gasped as his fingers pressed gently against her most intimate place, finding the bundle of nerves that had ached for attention since their first kiss.

"So responsive," he praised, circling the sensitive nub through the fabric. "So perfect."

Beatrice bit her lip to keep from crying out as pleasure unlike anything she had experienced coursed through her. Her own tentative explorations had been nothing compared to the skilled movements of James's fingers.

"More," she pleaded, not entirely sure what she was asking for.

Understanding her need, James slipped his hand beneath the slit in her drawers, finally touching her bare flesh. They both groaned at the contact—Beatrice at the exquisite sensation, James at finding her so wet and ready.

"You feel amazing," he murmured, exploring her folds with gentle but purposeful strokes. His finger circled her entrance without penetrating, respecting the boundaries they had tacitly established.

Instead, he concentrated his attention on the sensitive bud at the apex of her sex, alternating between direct stimulation and broader strokes. Each movement built the tension within her higher, winding her tighter toward something just beyond her understanding.

"James," she gasped, her hips beginning to move against his hand of their own accord. "I feel—I need—"

"I know, sweetheart," he soothed, increasing the pressure and speed of his strokes. "Just let go. Let it happen."

The rising tension within her had built to an almost unbearable level—a threshold of pleasure so intense it bordered on pain. For a moment, Beatrice hesitated at that edge, afraid of what lay beyond.

"Trust me," James whispered, capturing her mouth in a deep

kiss as his fingers moved with perfect precision.

The combination of his kiss and touch pushed her past the threshold. Pleasure exploded through her body in waves, radiating outward from where his fingers still moved against her. Her inner muscles contracted rhythmically as release washed over her, drawing a strangled cry from her throat that James captured with his mouth.

For endless moments, she shuddered against him, caught in the grip of sensations so intense she barely recognized herself. Only gradually did the waves recede, leaving her limp and trembling in his arms.

When she finally opened her eyes, she found James watching her with a mixture of tenderness and barely restrained desire. His arousal was evident in the tightness of his expression and the hardness still pressed against her hip, yet he made no move to seek his own release.

"That was..." she began, struggling to find words adequate to describe the experience.

"Beautiful," he finished for her. "You're extraordinary, Beatrice."

Awareness of her state of dishevelment suddenly struck her. Her dress was bunched around her waist, her breasts exposed, her legs splayed wantonly. Yet strangely, she felt no shame—only a languid satisfaction and growing curiosity.

"But you didn't..." she glanced meaningfully at the obvious bulge in his breeches.

A smile touched his lips. "This was about your pleasure, not mine."

Hesitantly, her hand moved to cover the evidence of his arousal. Even through the fabric, she could feel the impressive size and heat of him. "I want to learn," she said softly. "To give you what you've given me."

James's breath caught at her touch. For a moment, it seemed he might accept her offer. Then gently, he caught her wrist and brought her hand to his lips.

"Another time," he promised. "Tonight was for you."

Despite her lingering curiosity, Beatrice felt a rush of affection at his restraint. No man of her acquaintance would have denied himself release once offered, yet James seemed determined to keep their encounter focused on her pleasure alone.

With tender care, he helped her rearrange her clothing, even rebuttoning her bodice with surprising dexterity. When she was presentable once more, he pulled her into his arms for a long, slow kiss that held more emotion than mere passion.

"We should return to our chambers," he said reluctantly when they parted. "Dawn will come too soon."

Reality intruded on their private sanctuary. Tomorrow they would have to face the rest of the house party, maintain proper distance, pretend this moment of intimate connection had never occurred.

"What happens now?" she asked, suddenly uncertain. "Between us?"

His expression softened. "Whatever you wish, Beatrice. I would court you properly if you'll allow it. Or we can continue our more… private acquaintance. Or both."

The options were dizzying in their implications. Proper courtship meant public acknowledgment of his interest—something that would certainly reach her father's ears. It meant potential marriage, a complete change in her life's trajectory. Their private connection, on the other hand, offered pleasure without commitment but at significant risk to her reputation.

"I need time," she admitted. "To think."

"Of course." He helped her to her feet, steadying her when her legs proved still unsteady from her release. "Though I hope you know my preference already."

"And what is that?"

"Both," he said simply. "I want all of you, Beatrice—publicly and privately. But the choice must be yours."

The sincerity in his voice moved her deeply. This was not the calculated seduction of a rake but the genuine declaration of a man who had revealed as much of himself to her as she had to him.

"I'll think about it," she promised.

They left the library separately, James insisting on checking the corridors before allowing her to make her way back to her chamber. The journey seemed surreal after the intensity of their encounter—the same hallways and stairs she had traversed earlier now witness to her transformed state.

In her room, Beatrice slipped out of her dress and into her nightgown, still feeling the ghost of James's touch on her skin. As she lay in bed, her body hummed with lingering pleasure and new awareness. For the first time, she understood what the journal entries had described—the power of physical connection when combined with emotional resonance.

Sleep came easily, her dreams filled with blue eyes and gentle hands guiding her toward ever greater pleasure.

Chapter 6

Dawn brought clarity along with its gentle light. Beatrice awoke feeling changed in ways that went beyond the physical pleasure she had experienced. The vulnerability in James's eyes when he spoke of wanting "all of her" had affected her as deeply as his intimate touch.

As Frances helped her dress for breakfast in a morning gown of pale yellow muslin, Beatrice found herself studying her reflection in the mirror. Did she look different? Could others see the transformation she felt within? Her cheeks perhaps held more color, her eyes a brighter sparkle, but otherwise, she appeared the same bookish Lady Beatrice as before.

"You slept well, my lady?" Frances asked, arranging Beatrice's hair in a simple but becoming style. "You seem particularly refreshed this morning."

"Very well, thank you," Beatrice replied, hoping her blush would be attributed to the warmth of the room.

The breakfast room was already half full when she arrived. James stood by the window in conversation with Mrs. Thornfield, looking unfairly handsome in a morning coat of deep blue that emphasized his broad shoulders. At her entrance, his gaze immediately found hers, a subtle smile touching his lips before his expression returned to polite neutrality.

That small acknowledgment sent warmth spreading through her body. It was strange how differently she perceived him now—not just as the author of explicit journal entries or the notorious rake of London gossip, but as the man whose hands had brought her to ecstasy, whose eyes had watched her with tender admiration in her most vulnerable moment.

Thomas intercepted her before she could approach the breakfast table. "Good morning, Bea. I was beginning to think you'd sleep the day away."

"It's barely eight, Thomas," she pointed out, accepting a cup of tea from a footman.

"Late enough that I've already been for a ride and spoken to half the house party," he countered. "Including your Lord Ashworth."

She nearly choked on her tea. "He is not my Lord Ashworth, and what could you possibly have to discuss with him?"

Thomas's expression grew serious. "His intentions, of course. After your ride together and his obvious attention at charades last night, people are beginning to talk."

Alarm raced through her. "What did he say?"

"That he finds you fascinating and hopes to become better acquainted during our stay." Thomas studied her face carefully. "He also mentioned something curious about a shared interest in philosophy. I wasn't aware you had developed such scholarly inclinations."

Heat rushed to Beatrice's cheeks. That particular "shared interest" had led directly to their clandestine correspondence and last night's intimate encounter. "We've had several interesting conversations," she said vaguely.

"Hmm." Thomas didn't appear convinced. "Well, I've invited him to ride with us again this morning. The rain has cleared, and I thought we might visit those Roman ruins again. You seemed to enjoy them."

The prospect of spending time with James under her brother's watchful eye was both frustrating and exciting. At least they would be together, even if propriety demanded distance.

"That sounds lovely," she agreed, turning toward the breakfast buffet to hide her eagerness.

As she selected pastries and fruit for her plate, Caroline Blackwood appeared at her elbow. The blonde beauty wore a morning dress of pale pink that emphasized her voluptuous figure, her golden curls arranged in an elaborate style despite the early hour.

"Good morning, Lady Beatrice," Caroline said with false sweetness. "You look positively glowing today. Must be all that fresh air and... exercise."

The innuendo was clear, though Beatrice was certain Caroline couldn't know about last night's library encounter. "Good morning, Lady Caroline. Yes, country air does wonders for one's complexion."

Caroline's smile sharpened. "Indeed. Though I find certain activities even more beneficial for a woman's appearance. The flush of... satisfaction is unmistakable."

Before Beatrice could formulate a suitably cutting response, James approached their corner of the room. "Lady Beatrice, Lady Caroline," he greeted them with perfect politeness, though his eyes lingered on Beatrice. "I understand we're to ride to the ruins again this morning."

"So it seems," Caroline replied. "Though I wasn't included in the invitation."

"An oversight I'm sure could be rectified," James said smoothly, though something in his tone suggested he hoped otherwise.

Caroline's laugh held little humor. "No need. I promised Mrs. Thornfield I would help arrange flowers for tonight's masquerade. Perhaps another time."

As she swept away, James raised an eyebrow. "Masquerade?"

"Did you not hear? Mrs. Thornfield announced it last night during charades. A proper masked ball to celebrate the midpoint of the house party." Beatrice lowered her voice. "Convenient timing for us, wouldn't you say?"

His eyes darkened with understanding. "Indeed. Masks provide a certain… freedom from scrutiny."

The implications hung between them—the possibility of meeting less formally during the festivities, of stealing moments together under the guise of masked anonymity.

"Though my brother seems determined to act as my shadow," she added, nodding toward where Thomas watched them from across the room.

James smiled. "He's protective, not omniscient. And I've managed to navigate more complicated obstacles in the pursuit of worthwhile goals."

The casual reference to his rakish past should have bothered her, yet somehow it didn't. Perhaps because she had glimpsed the man beneath the reputation—a man capable of tenderness and restraint when it mattered.

"We should join the others," she said, conscious of curious glances from other guests. "Before gossip outpaces reality."

"Too late for that, I fear," he murmured as they moved toward the main breakfast table. "But let them talk. I have nothing to hide regarding my admiration for you."

The public acknowledgment of his interest sent a thrill through Beatrice that rivaled the physical sensations of the previous night. It was one thing to be desired in private, quite another to be openly admired by one of the most eligible bachelors in England.

* * *

The morning ride to the ruins passed pleasantly despite Thomas's obvious chaperoning efforts. James maintained impeccable propriety in his behavior toward Beatrice, though his eyes often conveyed messages far less proper when Thomas wasn't watching.

At the ruins, they dismounted to explore further than their previous visit had allowed. Thomas, his military background asserting itself, insisted on investigating a partially collapsed wall, leaving Beatrice and James briefly alone among the ancient stones.

"I dreamt of you last night," James murmured, standing close enough for private conversation yet far enough for propriety. "After our encounter."

Beatrice's pulse quickened. "What did you dream?"

His eyes darkened. "That we continued where we left off. That I showed you other ways pleasure can be given and received."

The explicit implication sent heat pooling between her thighs. "I dreamt of you as well," she admitted. "Though my imagination is limited by inexperience."

"A limitation easily remedied," he suggested, his voice dropping lower. "Tonight, perhaps? During the masquerade?"

She glanced toward where Thomas was examining some carving on a distant wall. "It would be dangerous."

"The best experiences often are," he countered with a smile. "Wear something blue—the color suits you. And find an excuse to visit the conservatory at eleven. The masks should provide adequate disguise from casual observers."

Before she could respond, Thomas rejoined them, and conversation necessarily returned to safer topics. Yet throughout their exploration and the ride back to Thornfield Estate, Beatrice found herself planning her costume and excuse for the evening's rendezvous.

* * *

Preparations for the masquerade consumed the afternoon. Mrs. Thornfield had apparently been planning the event for weeks, with costumes and masks available for guests who hadn't brought their own. The great ballroom was transformed with swaths of colorful fabric, hundreds of candles, and floral arrangements that perfumed the air.

In her chamber, Beatrice surveyed the options Frances had laid out on the bed. Among them was a gown of sapphire blue silk with silver embroidery that caught the light when it moved. The neckline was lower than Beatrice typically wore, with short puffed sleeves that would leave her arms mostly bare. It was daring without being scandalous—perfect for the evening's plans.

"This one, I think," she said, indicating the blue gown. "With the silver filigree mask."

Frances looked pleased with her selection. "An excellent

choice, my lady. The color will bring out your eyes beautifully."

As her maid helped her prepare, Beatrice found her thoughts returning to the library and James's skilled touch. What "other ways" of pleasure had he hinted at this morning? What might happen in the conservatory tonight if they managed to find privacy? The anticipation was both terrifying and thrilling.

By the time Frances had finished arranging her hair in an elaborate style with silver ribbons woven through the chestnut curls, Beatrice hardly recognized herself in the mirror. The blue gown enhanced her slim figure, the modest swell of her breasts rising above the neckline in a way that was alluring rather than vulgar. The silver mask, when tied in place, transformed her further—lending mystery to her familiar features and confidence to her bearing.

"You look magnificent, my lady," Frances said with genuine admiration. "Lord Ashworth won't be able to take his eyes off you."

Beatrice started at the mention of James. "What makes you think Lord Ashworth would particularly notice me?"

Frances smiled knowingly. "Begging your pardon, my lady, but the entire servants' hall is aware of his interest in you. His valet says he's been in unusually good spirits these past days."

The idea that their connection was the subject of belowstairs gossip should have mortified her. Instead, Beatrice found herself childishly pleased that James's behavior had changed noticeably enough for his servants to remark upon it.

"Well, we'll see," she said noncommittally, though excitement fluttered in her stomach at the prospect of their planned meeting.

Chapter 7

The masquerade was in full swing when Beatrice entered the ballroom. The combination of masks, elaborate costumes, and strategically dimmed lighting created an atmosphere of mystery and possibility. Normally reserved gentlemen seemed bolder behind their disguises, while ladies permitted liberties of conversation that would be scandalous in normal circumstances.

Thomas, easily identifiable despite his black mask by his military bearing and fair hair, immediately approached her. "There you are, Bea. I almost didn't recognize you. You look…" He paused, seemingly surprised by her transformation. "Different."

"That's rather the point of a masquerade, isn't it?" she replied lightly. "The freedom to be someone else for an evening."

His expression turned suspicious. "Just don't use that freedom unwisely. Masked or not, reputation matters."

Before she could reassure him, Mrs. Thornfield approached with a gentleman Beatrice didn't immediately recognize. He wore an elaborate mask of silver and midnight blue that matched her own, his tall figure clothed in a perfectly tailored evening suit of deep blue. Only when he bowed did she realize it was James—his movements unmistakable despite the disguise.

"Ah, Lady Beatrice! I was just telling Lord Ashworth how striking you look this evening," Mrs. Thornfield said with a knowing smile. "The blue suits you admirably."

"Thank you, Mrs. Thornfield," Beatrice replied, dipping into a curtsy. "Lord Ashworth, good evening."

"Lady Beatrice." His voice held perfect composure, though his eyes behind the mask conveyed an entirely different message. "Would you honor me with a dance? I believe they're forming sets for the next quadrille."

Thomas looked as if he might object, but Mrs. Thornfield smoothly intervened. "Captain Harrington, I simply must introduce you to Lady Sarah Berkeley. Her brother serves in your regiment, I believe."

As their hostess deftly steered Thomas away, James offered his arm to Beatrice. "Shall we?"

The touch of his hand as he guided her to the dance floor sent electricity through her body. Even this small contact seemed charged with significance after the intimacy they had shared.

"You look breathtaking," he murmured as they took their positions for the quadrille. "That color against your skin... I can't stop thinking about how it would look pooled on the floor around your feet."

The boldness of his statement made her cheeks flame beneath her mask. "James! Someone might hear you."

His smile was visible even behind his disguise. "That's the beauty of a masquerade, my dear. Everyone is too concerned with their own intrigues to pay attention to ours."

Chapter 7

The dance began, forcing them to separate and move through the patterns with other partners. Each time they came together again, however briefly, the tension between them intensified. By the dance's conclusion, Beatrice found herself breathless more from anticipation than exertion.

As custom dictated, James escorted her from the floor once the music ended. Instead of returning her to Thomas's side, however, he guided her toward the refreshment table positioned near doors leading to a terrace.

"Still planning to meet me later?" he asked quietly, handing her a glass of champagne.

"Yes," she replied, the single syllable a commitment to whatever might follow. "Though I'm not sure how to excuse myself without raising suspicion."

"Leave that to me," he said confidently. "I've arranged a small distraction around half past ten. When it occurs, make your way to the conservatory. I'll join you shortly thereafter."

The casual competence with which he planned their rendezvous both impressed and unsettled her. This was clearly not his first clandestine meeting—a reminder of his experienced past that pricked at her confidence.

Sensing her hesitation, James touched her wrist lightly. "What troubles you?"

"Nothing," she said automatically, then reconsidered. Honesty had defined their relationship thus far; why abandon it now? "Actually, I was thinking about your expertise in arranging such meetings. It's a reminder of how different our experiences are."

Instead of dismissing her concern, he considered it seriously. "Does that bother you? My past?"

"It shouldn't," she admitted. "What happened before we met

has nothing to do with what happens between us now. And yet..."

"You wonder if you're merely another conquest," he finished for her, his voice gentle rather than defensive. "Another name in a lengthy list."

Put so bluntly, the fear seemed both valid and absurd. "Yes," she whispered.

James glanced around to ensure they weren't overheard, then leaned closer. "Beatrice, from the moment I found your note in my journal, you became something entirely different from anyone who came before. Those experiences—numerous as they were—never involved the connection of minds that preceded physical touch. They never included the vulnerability of revealing my private thoughts first, my body second."

The sincerity in his voice moved her deeply. "I want to believe that."

"Then do," he said simply. "Or better yet, judge me by my actions from this point forward, not by rumors of my past."

Before she could respond, Thomas appeared at her side, his expression difficult to read behind his mask but his posture radiating displeasure.

"Bea, Mother's friend Lady Essex is asking after you," he said, deliberately using their childhood nickname to emphasize their connection. "Lord Ashworth, I believe Lady Caroline was looking for you earlier."

The pointed reference to Caroline was clearly meant to create distance between them. James, however, merely smiled politely.

"I'm sure Lady Caroline will find me if her need is pressing," he replied smoothly. "Lady Beatrice, thank you for the dance and conversation. Perhaps another later this evening?"

His eyes held a private message that made her pulse quicken

despite her brother's watchful presence. "I would enjoy that, my lord."

As James departed with a formal bow, Thomas turned to her with evident frustration. "Must you encourage him so openly? Half the room is talking about how much time you've spent together."

"We danced once and shared a brief conversation," she pointed out. "Hardly a scandal."

"It's not just tonight," Thomas insisted, guiding her toward a group of older ladies across the room. "It's the cumulative effect of your rides together, your private conversations, the way you look at each other. People notice these things, Bea."

Guilt pricked at her conscience. If Thomas was this concerned about their public interactions, how would he react to knowing what had occurred in the library? Or what she planned for later tonight?

"I'm not a child, Thomas," she said with more confidence than she felt. "I'm three and twenty, well past the age of making my own decisions about gentlemen's attentions."

"Being of age doesn't guarantee wisdom," he countered. "Father entrusted me with your welfare while he's abroad. What would he say if he knew you were encouraging the most notorious rake in London?"

The question hung uncomfortably between them as they reached Lady Essex, forcing Beatrice to paste on a smile and engage in polite conversation while her mind remained fixed on the approaching hour and her planned meeting with James.

* * *

The ballroom grew warmer and more crowded as the evening

progressed. Beatrice danced with several gentlemen, careful to accept only one more invitation from James to avoid further provoking Thomas's suspicions. Each time they passed in the patterns of the dance, however, the anticipation between them built higher.

At precisely half past ten, a commotion erupted near the main entrance to the ballroom. A footman had apparently tripped while carrying a tray of champagne, sending glass shattering across the marble floor and splashing several guests. As attention turned toward the disruption, Beatrice seized her opportunity.

Slipping through the French doors onto the terrace, she made her way along the stone balustrade toward the conservatory attached to the east wing of Thornfield Estate. The night air felt cool against her flushed skin, the distant sounds of the orchestra fading as she moved farther from the ballroom.

The conservatory stood like a crystal palace in the moonlight, its glass walls and ceiling capturing the ethereal glow. Inside, exotic plants from Mrs. Thornfield's extensive collection created a private jungle, with winding paths disappearing among palm fronds and flowering vines.

Beatrice hesitated at the entrance, suddenly uncertain. What she was about to do went far beyond their written correspondence or even their encounter in the library. This was a deliberately planned assignation—the behavior of a woman with no regard for propriety or reputation.

Or perhaps, she thought with newfound boldness, *the behavior of a woman who values authentic connection over artificial constraints.*

With that thought firmly in mind, she pushed open the glass door and entered the conservatory. The air inside was warm and humid, heavy with the scent of jasmine and other night-blooming flowers. Lanterns had been strategically placed along the paths, creating pools of golden light amid the shadows.

Beatrice wandered deeper into the verdant space, her blue silk gown brushing against leaves and fronds as she passed. The exotic setting felt appropriate for what might transpire—removed from the rigid structures of society, surrounded by nature's untamed beauty.

"You came."

James's voice from behind her made her turn. He had discarded his mask, his handsome face no longer obscured as he approached from between two towering palms. His evening attire remained impeccable, though he had loosened his cravat slightly in concession to the conservatory's warmth.

"Did you doubt I would?" she asked, reaching up to untie her own mask. If he was brave enough to show his true face, she would do the same.

"I hoped rather than doubted," he replied, watching as she removed the silver filigree that had concealed her features. "Though your brother's vigilance gave me pause."

"Thomas means well," she said, setting her mask on a nearby stone bench. "He's protective because he loves me."

"As he should be." James moved closer, close enough that she could detect his familiar scent of sandalwood and something uniquely him. "If you were my sister, I would lock you away from men like me."

The self-deprecating humor made her smile despite her nervousness. "Then I'm grateful you're not my brother."

"As am I," he murmured, reaching out to trace the line of her jaw with gentle fingers. "Though 'grateful' seems an inadequate word for what I feel when I look at you."

The simple touch sent anticipation spiraling through her body. After the restraint they had shown all evening—indeed, all day—even this small contact felt intensely intimate.

"Your distraction worked perfectly," she said, trying to maintain composure despite her racing pulse. "Though I feel sorry for the footman who sacrificed his dignity for our assignation."

James's smile turned mischievous. "Don't be. He was handsomely compensated, and the glasses were empty. Mrs. Thornfield was informed in advance and thought it a small price for a bit of drama."

"Mrs. Thornfield knows?" Beatrice asked, alarmed.

"Not specifically what we planned," he assured her. "Only that I wished to create a diversion for a private conversation. She's more… understanding of such matters than most hostesses."

The implication that their hostess might tacitly approve of their meeting should have reassured her. Instead, it underscored the impropriety of what they were doing—conspiring with servants, manipulating circumstances, all for a few moments alone together.

James seemed to sense her hesitation. "We can return to the ballroom if you've reconsidered," he offered. "No expectations, no disappointment. The choice is entirely yours, Beatrice."

The sincerity in his voice decided her. This man—who could have any woman he desired, who had proven his skill and confidence in intimate matters—was placing her comfort above his own desires. It was this consideration, more than his handsome face or skilled touch, that cemented her decision.

"I don't want to return," she said firmly. "I want to be here, with you."

Relief and desire mingled in his expression as he closed the remaining distance between them. "May I kiss you then?"

Chapter 7

"Please," she whispered, already tilting her face up to meet his.

Their lips came together with the pent-up longing of the entire day spent in forced propriety. What began as a gentle reunion quickly deepened into something more urgent, more primal. James's arms encircled her waist, pulling her against his body as his tongue sought entrance to her mouth.

Beatrice yielded willingly, her hands moving up to tangle in his dark hair as she had longed to do since their library encounter. The texture was as silky as she remembered, sliding between her fingers as she held him to her.

When they finally broke apart for air, both were breathing heavily. "You have no idea how difficult it was to maintain proper distance today," James confessed, his voice rough with desire. "All I could think about was touching you again, hearing those soft sounds you make when pleasure overtakes you."

His explicit words sent heat rushing to Beatrice's core. "I thought of little else myself," she admitted. "Especially after your hints this morning about... other ways of experiencing pleasure."

A slow smile spread across his face at her boldness. "Are you asking me to demonstrate, Lady Beatrice?"

"I believe I am, Lord Ashworth," she replied, surprising herself with her forthrightness.

His eyes darkened with desire as he guided her deeper into the conservatory, toward a secluded alcove where climbing roses surrounded a padded bench. The space was perfectly private, hidden from the main paths by strategically planted greenery.

"Here," he said, his voice low and intimate in the enclosed space. "We're unlikely to be disturbed."

The reality of what they were about to do sent both trepidation and excitement coursing through Beatrice. They were still within the main house, separated from the ballroom by only a few hundred yards. Discovery would mean complete ruin.

Yet as James's hands came to rest lightly on her shoulders, all thoughts of consequences faded. His touch was gentle but confident as he turned her slightly, his fingers finding the buttons that secured the back of her gown.

"May I?" he asked, his breath warm against her ear.

She nodded, not trusting her voice as his fingers began to work the small fastenings. Each button released sent a shiver down her spine—partly from the cool air touching newly exposed skin, partly from the intimacy of being undressed by another.

"Your skin is like silk," he murmured, pressing his lips to her shoulder as it was revealed. "I've dreamt of seeing more of it since our night in the library."

The gown loosened as the last button yielded to his skilled fingers. With careful movements, he eased it forward over her shoulders, helping her step out of it as it pooled around her feet in exactly the way he had described earlier. The heavy silk made a soft shushing sound as it settled on the stone floor.

Beatrice stood before him in only her undergarments—the thin chemise that barely concealed her breasts, her corset less restrictive than formal occasions required but still emphasizing her narrow waist, and drawers that ended just below her knees. Silk stockings encased her legs, held up by garters tied with blue ribbons to match her gown.

James stepped back slightly, his gaze traveling over her partially clad form with undisguised appreciation. "Exquisite," he breathed. "Even more beautiful than I imagined."

Chapter 7

Self-consciousness warred with pride at his evident admiration. No man had ever seen her in such a state of undress; the vulnerability was both frightening and thrilling.

"Your turn," she said softly, finding courage in his desire.

His eyebrows rose in surprise at her boldness, but he made no objection as her fingers moved to his cravat, carefully untying the intricate knot. The fine white fabric came away in her hands, exposing the strong column of his throat.

Next came his evening coat, which she pushed from his broad shoulders with newfound confidence. The waistcoat followed, her fingers fumbling slightly with the small buttons in her eagerness.

When she reached for his shirt, however, he caught her hands gently. "Not yet," he murmured. "Tonight is still about your pleasure, Beatrice. Let me show you something new."

Before she could question his meaning, he guided her to sit on the padded bench, then knelt before her on the stone floor. The position was startlingly intimate—James Ashworth, Earl of Westmoreland, on his knees before her like a supplicant.

His hands moved to her ankles, where he slowly removed her satin slippers. Then, with deliberate gentleness, his fingers began to trace upward along her stockinged calf.

"Do you recall the entry you first read?" he asked, his voice low and intimate. "About the widow in the library?"

Heat flooded Beatrice's cheeks as she remembered the explicit description of him pleasuring a woman with his mouth. "Yes," she whispered.

"I want to do that for you," he said, his eyes holding hers as his hands continued their upward journey. "To taste you, to bring you pleasure in a way you've likely never imagined."

The suggestion was so shocking, so far beyond the boundaries of what Beatrice had considered possible, that she momentarily lost her voice. Such an act seemed impossibly intimate—more so even than what propriety deemed the ultimate intimacy.

"You can refuse," he added softly, correctly interpreting her silence. "As I've said from the beginning, nothing happens without your consent."

The consideration in his voice, the patience with which he awaited her decision, tipped the balance from uncertainty to curiosity. "I trust you," she said finally. "Show me."

Relief and desire mingled in his expression as his hands resumed their exploration, moving higher to find the ribbons securing her garters. With careful precision, he untied one, then the other, before rolling each stocking slowly down her leg.

The sensation of his fingers against her bare skin was exquisite—each touch sending sparks of anticipation through her body. When both stockings had been removed, he pressed a kiss to the inside of her right ankle, then began a slow ascent up her calf, placing kisses at intervals as he went.

By the time he reached her knee, Beatrice was trembling with anticipation. The feeling of his lips and occasionally his tongue against her skin was unlike anything she had experienced, each contact sending pulses of heat directly to her core.

"May I?" he asked again, his hands hovering at the waistband of her drawers.

She nodded, lifting her hips slightly to allow him to slide the garment down her legs. The air felt cool against her most intimate places as the final barrier was removed, leaving her exposed to his gaze despite the chemise and loosened corset she still wore.

James's eyes darkened as he looked at her, his expression one of reverent desire rather than mere lust. "You are perfection," he murmured, his hands gently encouraging her knees to part.

Beatrice bit her lip, torn between modesty and the building need his touches had awakened. Desire won, her thighs slowly opening to his gaze.

"Beautiful," he whispered, lowering his head to place a kiss on the inside of her thigh, dangerously close to where heat and dampness betrayed her arousal.

His mouth moved higher, leaving a trail of kisses that made her breath come faster. When he finally reached the apex of her thighs, he paused, looking up to meet her eyes one last time in silent question.

At her nod, he lowered his head and placed his mouth directly against her center.

The first touch of his tongue sent a shock of pleasure so intense that Beatrice gasped aloud, her hands flying to his hair instinctively. The sensation was unlike anything she had experienced—more immediate, more overwhelming than even his skilled fingers had been in the library.

"James," she breathed, unsure whether she was pleading for him to stop or continue.

He responded by deepening his attentions, his tongue finding and circling the sensitive bud that was the center of her pleasure. One hand moved to her hip, steadying her as she began to move against his mouth unconsciously.

The intimate knowledge he demonstrated was both shocking and thrilling—each stroke of his tongue seemed perfectly calibrated to build her pleasure higher. When he added the gentle suction of his lips, Beatrice had to bite back a cry that would surely have been heard beyond their alcove.

"Let go," he murmured against her sensitive flesh. "Trust me."

His tongue returned to its relentless rhythm, and Beatrice felt herself climbing rapidly toward that now-familiar precipice. This time, however, the intensity was magnified tenfold, her entire body drawn tight as a bowstring as pleasure built to an almost unbearable peak.

When release came, it crashed through her with such force that she had to muffle her cry against her own arm. Wave after wave of ecstasy radiated outward from where James's mouth still moved against her, gentling his attentions as she shuddered through the aftershocks.

Only when the last tremor had subsided did he lift his head, his expression one of masculine satisfaction as he took in her flushed face and dazed eyes. Slowly, deliberately, he wiped his mouth with the back of his hand—a gesture that should have shocked her but instead sent a renewed pulse of heat through her still-sensitive body.

"Now you understand why poets call it 'little death,'" he said softly, rising to sit beside her on the bench. "For a moment, everything else ceases to exist."

Beatrice was still struggling to form coherent thoughts, her body languid with pleasure even as her mind reeled from the intimacy they had shared. "I never imagined..." she began, then stopped, unsure how to articulate the transformation she felt.

"Few women are permitted to imagine," he replied, tucking a strand of hair behind her ear with gentle fingers. "Society ensures your education excludes the very knowledge your body craves."

The truth of his statement struck her forcefully. Her entire upbringing had been designed to keep her ignorant of these matters—as if knowledge itself would somehow taint her virtue rather than enhance her understanding.

"Thank you," she said finally, the simple words inadequate for the gift he had given her. "For showing me."

His smile was tender rather than triumphant. "The pleasure was mutual, I assure you."

Her gaze dropped to where his trousers showed clear evidence of his arousal, and she felt a surge of boldness born of the intimacy they had shared. "Let me return the favor," she suggested, her hand moving to rest on his thigh.

For a moment, he seemed tempted. Then, with evident reluctance, he covered her hand with his own. "Another time," he said. "We've already risked much tonight, and your absence from the ballroom will soon be noted."

Disappointment warred with the knowledge that he was right. They had already stayed longer than prudence dictated.

"Will there be another time?" she asked as he helped her back into her gown, his fingers nimble with the buttons as they had been removing them.

"If you wish it," he replied, retrieving her mask from where it lay forgotten on the bench. "Though perhaps in a less precarious setting."

As she pinned her slightly disheveled hair back into some semblance of order, a thought occurred to her. "The journal—will we continue writing to each other as well?"

James smiled as he retied his cravat. "Words and actions complement each other, don't they? I see no reason to abandon what brought us together."

Once they were both presentable—or as presentable as circumstances allowed—James took her hands in his. "We should return separately. I'll go first and make sure the path is clear."

Before leaving, however, he pulled her close for one more

kiss—this one gentle and lingering, filled with something deeper than mere physical desire. When they parted, Beatrice found herself wishing they could remain in their private jungle, away from society's judgmental eyes and restrictive rules.

"Until tomorrow," he murmured, placing a final kiss on her forehead before disappearing down the winding path toward the conservatory entrance.

Alone in the alcove, Beatrice took a moment to collect herself. The woman who had entered the conservatory an hour ago was not the same one preparing to leave. Knowledge had transformed her—not just carnal knowledge, but understanding of her own desires and capacity for pleasure.

Society would call me ruined, she thought as she replaced her mask and checked her appearance one last time. *Yet I feel more complete than ever before.*

With that realization firmly in mind, she followed the path back toward the ballroom, where masks of a different sort awaited.

Chapter 8

The final days of the Thornfield house party brought an unexpected complication: rain. Not the gentle showers of previous days, but torrential downpours that confined the guests to the main house and limited opportunities for private encounters. The forced proximity created its own tension as Beatrice and James maintained proper distance in public while exchanging heated glances when no one was watching.

Their correspondence through the journal continued, however, with increasingly explicit exchanges that left Beatrice flushed and restless each night. James described in exquisite detail what he wished to do when they next found privacy, while Beatrice surprised herself with the boldness of her responses. The written word provided a freedom that face-to-face conversation could not—allowing her to express desires she was still learning to name.

On the morning of the final full day of the house party, Beatrice woke early, determined to visit the library before breakfast. The rain continued to lash against her windows as

Frances helped her dress in a simple morning gown of lavender muslin with a higher neckline than she had favored recently—a concession to the cooler weather rather than a return to her former modesty.

"Will you be joining the others for breakfast, my lady?" Frances asked as she arranged Beatrice's hair in a simple chignon.

"Eventually," Beatrice replied. "I thought I might visit the library first. There's a book I've been meaning to return."

Frances's knowing smile suggested she wasn't fooled by the excuse, but she merely said, "Of course, my lady. Shall I come find you when the breakfast bell rings?"

"That won't be necessary," Beatrice assured her. "I can keep track of the time."

Once alone, she retrieved the journal from its hiding place beneath her mattress. After their encounter in the conservatory, James had suggested she keep it in her chamber rather than returning it to the library panel—both for convenience and to reduce the risk of discovery by servants or other guests.

The leather-bound volume had become precious to her over the past week—not just for the explicit exchanges it contained, but for the insights into James's mind it provided. Beyond the sexual content, he had revealed his thoughts on literature, philosophy, and society's constraints. She had responded in kind, sharing perspectives she rarely voiced in proper company for fear of being labeled a bluestocking or worse.

Their intellectual connection had deepened alongside the physical, creating a bond that increasingly felt like something dangerously close to love—a realization that both thrilled and terrified her.

The corridors were quiet as she made her way to the library, most guests still abed after a late night of indoor entertainment. Mrs. Thornfield had arranged an impromptu concert followed by card games to compensate for the inability to venture outdoors, and the festivities had continued well past midnight.

Beatrice had hoped to find the library empty, giving her time to leave the journal and perhaps a final note before breakfast. To her surprise, however, she found James already there, standing by the window watching the rain cascade down the glass.

He turned at the sound of the door, his face lighting with pleasure when he saw her. "Beatrice. I had hoped you might come early."

The simple joy in his expression warmed her more effectively than the small fire burning in the grate. He looked particularly handsome this morning, dressed in a charcoal gray morning coat that emphasized his broad shoulders and dark gray breeches that showcased his muscular thighs. His cravat was tied in a simple style that drew attention to his strong jawline, now clean-shaven for the day ahead.

"Great minds think alike, it seems," she replied, closing the door behind her but leaving it slightly ajar for propriety's sake. "I brought the journal."

James crossed to meet her, taking the leather-bound volume from her hands. Their fingers brushed in the exchange, sending the now-familiar spark of awareness through her body.

"Your latest entry was... most inspiring," he said, his voice dropping to that intimate register that never failed to make her pulse quicken. "I found myself unable to sleep after reading it."

Heat rose to Beatrice's cheeks as she recalled what she had written—a detailed fantasy of what she wished to do to him, inspired by his descriptions of pleasure given and received. "It seems my literary education has taken an unexpected turn under your tutelage."

His smile held both amusement and heat. "You're a remarkably quick study. Though I confess I'm eager to move beyond theory to more practical applications of your knowledge."

The implication was clear, and Beatrice felt answering desire pool in her core. "The rain complicates matters," she observed. "Privacy is in short supply when everyone is confined indoors."

"True," he conceded, setting the journal on a nearby table and moving closer to her. "Though I've been considering alternatives."

"Such as?" she asked, conscious of his proximity and the effect it had on her body—her breasts tightening beneath her corset, her breathing growing shallow.

James glanced toward the door, confirming it remained ajar, then lowered his voice further. "Mrs. Thornfield has invited me to extend my stay beyond the official conclusion of the house party. I had thought to accept and suggest that perhaps your brother might be persuaded to do the same."

The possibility of additional days at Thornfield sent a thrill through Beatrice. "Thomas is eager to return to London," she said. "He has regimental duties awaiting him."

"But you could perhaps express a desire to remain longer? Mrs. Thornfield would certainly support the idea. She's grown quite fond of you."

The suggestion was tempting—dangerously so. "To stay without Thomas would raise eyebrows," she pointed out. "An unmarried lady remaining without proper chaperone..."

"Mrs. Thornfield herself would serve as chaperone," James countered. "And her reputation is beyond reproach."

"While her discretion appears equally beyond question," Beatrice added with a small smile. "She seems remarkably willing to facilitate our... friendship."

James's expression turned more serious. "Eleanor Thornfield had her own great love affair in her youth. It ended tragically—he died before they could marry—but she has always maintained that those few months of happiness were worth a lifetime of proper solitude."

The revelation about their hostess cast the older woman's knowing smiles and strategic interventions in a new light. "You seem well-acquainted with her history."

"She was my mother's closest friend," he explained. "After my father died and my mother followed a year later, Eleanor became something of a surrogate parent. She's one of the few people who knows the man behind the reputation society has assigned me."

This glimpse into James's past—the orphaned boy behind the controlled man—touched Beatrice deeply. "I'm sorry about your parents," she said softly. "How old were you when you lost them?"

"Seventeen when my father died, eighteen when my mother followed," he replied, a shadow crossing his handsome features. "Old enough to inherit everything except the guidance I still needed."

Beatrice could see how such early loss might have shaped him—pushing him toward physical pleasures that required no emotional vulnerability, keeping deeper connections at bay. "Is that when your reputation began?"

He nodded, moving to stand by the fireplace. "Grief and fortune are a dangerous combination in a young man. I sought distraction in all the ways society permits men of privilege—gambling, drinking, women. By the time I recognized the emptiness of such pursuits, my reputation was firmly established."

"And the journal?" she asked. "When did that begin?"

"Three years ago," he said, turning back to face her. "After a particularly hollow encounter with a widow who knew exactly what she wanted and cared nothing for who I was beyond my title and bed skills. I found myself writing about the experience—not just the physical details, but the emptiness that followed. It became a habit, then a compulsion. A way to make sense of experiences that increasingly felt meaningless."

The vulnerability in his admission moved her. This was the man she had glimpsed in the journal pages—thoughtful, self-aware, yearning for connection beyond the physical.

"Until I found it," she said softly.

"Until you found it," he agreed, his expression warming. "And had the courage to respond not just to the explicit content but to the loneliness between the lines."

He moved toward her again, close enough that she could feel the heat of his body without actually touching. "These past days with you, Beatrice—both in person and through our written exchanges—have meant more to me than I can adequately express. You've seen me—truly seen me—in a way no one has before."

The naked emotion in his voice made her heart ache with answering feeling. "As you have seen me," she whispered. "Beyond the bookish spinster, beyond society's limitations on what a woman should desire or express."

His hand rose to cup her cheek, his thumb tracing the curve of her lower lip in a gesture that had become familiar yet lost none of its power to affect her. "I don't want this to end when the house party concludes," he said, his voice low and intense. "Whatever happens today, I want you to know that."

Chapter 8

Before she could respond, the sound of voices in the corridor made them step apart quickly. James moved to the bookshelves as if searching for a volume, while Beatrice turned toward the window, both adopting poses of casual interest just as the library door opened fully.

Caroline Blackwood entered, her golden curls perfectly arranged despite the early hour, her morning dress of pale pink silk cut lower than fashion dictated for daytime. Her blue eyes narrowed as she took in the tableau before her.

"Lady Beatrice, Lord Ashworth," she greeted them, her voice sweet with underlying venom. "How surprising to find you both here so early. And alone."

"Hardly alone with the door open, Lady Caroline," James replied smoothly. "Lady Beatrice was kind enough to recommend a volume on Roman architecture after our visits to the ruins."

Caroline's perfect smile didn't reach her eyes. "How educational your friendship has proved to be. Though I wonder what other lessons have been exchanged between literature and architecture."

The insinuation hung in the air, impossible to miss. Beatrice felt heat rise to her cheeks, though whether from embarrassment or anger at Caroline's intrusion, she couldn't be sure.

"Knowledge takes many forms, Lady Caroline," she replied with more composure than she felt. "Some appreciate its pursuit more than others."

James moved casually toward the table where he had placed the journal, his body strategically blocking it from Caroline's view. "Was there something specific you were seeking in the library this morning?" he asked, his tone polite but dismissive.

Caroline's gaze flicked between them, calculation evident in her expression. "Actually, yes. I was looking for something… private. Something I believe may have been misplaced." Her eyes fixed on Beatrice. "Or perhaps taken by someone with an excessive interest in other people's possessions."

The direct reference to the journal sent alarm racing through Beatrice. Somehow, Caroline knew—or at least suspected—the nature of their secret correspondence.

"I can't imagine what you mean," Beatrice said, fighting to keep her voice steady.

"No?" Caroline moved further into the room, her gaze sweeping the shelves and tables as if searching for something specific. "How strange. I distinctly recall seeing a particular leather-bound volume in this very room some days ago. Small, unmarked, with contents of a… personal nature."

James's expression remained neutral, though Beatrice noticed his posture tense slightly. "Many books in a library this size might fit that description, Lady Caroline. Perhaps you could be more specific about the subject matter?"

Caroline's smile turned predatory. "Oh, the subject was quite… explicit, Lord Ashworth. Detailed accounts of encounters that would make even the most worldly person blush." Her gaze shifted to Beatrice. "Though apparently some find such material educational rather than shocking."

Before either could respond, the library door opened again to admit Thomas Harrington. His expression darkened as he took in the tableau—Beatrice by the window, James near the table, and Caroline looking like a cat who had cornered two particularly interesting mice.

"There you are, Bea," Thomas said, moving immediately to his sister's side. "I was concerned when your maid said you'd gone to the library alone."

Chapter 8

"Not alone, as you can see," Caroline observed sweetly. "Though perhaps she wished to be."

Thomas's jaw tightened. "Lady Caroline, would you excuse us? I need to speak with my sister privately."

"Of course," Caroline agreed with false graciousness. "Though you might wish to inquire about what your sister has been reading lately. Her literary tastes have developed in... interesting directions."

With a final pointed look at the table where the journal lay partially concealed by James's position, Caroline swept from the room, leaving an uncomfortable silence in her wake.

Thomas looked from Beatrice to James, suspicion evident in his expression. "What was that about?"

"Lady Caroline enjoys creating discord," James said smoothly. "A common trait among those who find genuine connection elusive."

"And what 'genuine connection' might you be forming with my sister in a deserted library before breakfast?" Thomas demanded, his protective instincts clearly roused.

Beatrice moved to intercede before the situation escalated. "Thomas, please. Lord Ashworth was merely assisting me in locating a book on Roman architecture after our visits to the ruins. There's nothing improper occurring."

The lie felt bitter on her tongue, especially when Thomas's expression made it clear he wasn't entirely convinced. "Then you won't mind if I escort you to breakfast now," he said. "Mrs. Thornfield has announced it will be served early today, as several guests are departing immediately after due to the weather."

Beatrice glanced at James, who gave her an almost imperceptible nod. "Of course," she agreed. "I've found what I was looking for."

As Thomas guided her toward the door with a proprietary hand on her elbow, she risked one last glance back. James had casually picked up the journal, sliding it into his coat pocket with a practiced movement that Thomas, focused on Beatrice, didn't notice.

Their eyes met briefly, his conveying a clear message: *This isn't over. We'll find another way.*

The promise sustained her as Thomas led her from the library, his lecture about propriety and reputation washing over her like the rain against the windows—persistent but ultimately unable to dampen the warmth James had kindled within her.

Chapter 9

Breakfast passed in a blur of tension, with Caroline making pointed remarks that sailed over most guests' heads but landed with precision for their intended targets. Thomas maintained a vigilant position beside Beatrice, effectively preventing any private communication with James, who sat at the opposite end of the table engaged in conversation with Mrs. Thornfield.

As the meal concluded, their hostess rose to address the gathering. "Given the inclement weather and the difficult travel conditions it has created, I wish to extend an invitation to any guests who would prefer to postpone their departure. Thornfield Estate is at your disposal for as long as the conditions warrant caution."

Several guests immediately accepted, expressing relief at not having to brave the muddy roads. James, as Beatrice had expected, was among them.

"I would be grateful to impose on your hospitality a few days longer, Mrs. Thornfield," he said. "My estate in Derbyshire will likely be even more affected by these rains, making travel north particularly challenging."

Their hostess smiled warmly. "No imposition at all, James. You know you're always welcome." Her gaze shifted to include Beatrice and Thomas. "Captain Harrington, Lady Beatrice—I do hope you'll consider extending your stay as well. The weather report suggests conditions may improve by week's end."

Before Thomas could decline, Beatrice spoke up. "That's most generous, Mrs. Thornfield. I would be delighted to accept, though I understand my brother has regimental duties awaiting him in London."

Thomas looked startled by her quick response. "Bea, we discussed returning together. Father would expect—"

"Father would expect me to avoid unnecessary risks," she countered smoothly. "The roads to London will be treacherous after such rain, and we've already received word that the bridge at Millford was threatening to flood yesterday." This last part was an invention, but delivered with such conviction that Thomas hesitated.

Mrs. Thornfield nodded gravely. "Indeed, several of my tenants reported the same. Most concerning. Captain Harrington, while I would never presume to interfere with your military obligations, perhaps your sister might remain here under my chaperonage until conditions improve? I assure you, her reputation would be perfectly safe in my care."

Thomas looked torn, glancing between Beatrice's hopeful expression and James's carefully neutral one. "I suppose if Mrs. Thornfield is willing to assume responsibility..." he began reluctantly.

"Splendid!" their hostess declared before he could reconsider. "Then it's settled. Those departing should prepare to leave within the hour to make the most of daylight, while those remaining can look forward to a more intimate gathering this evening."

As the breakfast party dispersed, Thomas pulled Beatrice aside. "Are you certain about this, Bea? It's not like you to separate from family, especially in unfamiliar surroundings."

"Thornfield hardly feels unfamiliar now," she pointed out. "And Mrs. Thornfield has been kindness itself. Besides, I've been enjoying the library tremendously." At least that part wasn't a lie.

Thomas's expression remained troubled. "This wouldn't have anything to do with Ashworth remaining as well, would it?"

The direct question caught her off guard. "Why would you think that?"

"Because I'm not blind, Beatrice," he said quietly. "I've seen how you look at each other. And this morning in the library... there was tension I couldn't quite identify."

Guilt pricked at her conscience. Thomas had always been perceptive, and their closeness made deceiving him particularly difficult. "Lord Ashworth is interesting company," she admitted carefully. "He's well-read and thoughtful—different from his public reputation."

"Men earn their reputations for a reason," Thomas insisted. "And his is particularly concerning where ladies are involved."

"People can change," she said softly. "Or perhaps they were never fully what rumors claimed to begin with."

Thomas studied her face for a long moment. "You're falling in love with him," he said finally, the words a statement rather than a question.

Beatrice couldn't bring herself to deny it, though she hadn't fully admitted the depth of her feelings even to herself until that moment. "Would that be so terrible?" she asked instead.

Her brother's expression softened. "Not if his intentions are honorable and his regard genuine. But Bea, men like Ashworth often view intelligent, bookish women as a challenge—a novel conquest rather than a lifelong companion."

The echo of her own earlier fears made Beatrice flinch slightly. "You don't know him," she said defensively.

"Neither do you, not really," Thomas countered. "A week of conversation, however stimulating, doesn't reveal a man's true character or intentions."

If only you knew, she thought, thinking of the journal and the intimate insights it had provided into James's mind and heart. Aloud, she said only, "I'm not a naive debutante, Thomas. I'm three and twenty, and I've had ample opportunity to observe men's motivations and methods."

He sighed, clearly recognizing her determination. "I can't force you to return with me, but promise me you'll be careful. And remember that a man worth having will respect your virtue and reputation."

The irony of his concern, given what had already transpired between her and James, almost made Beatrice laugh. Instead, she squeezed her brother's hand reassuringly. "I promise to guard both carefully."

Thomas didn't look entirely convinced, but he nodded reluctantly. "I'll write to Father from London, explaining that the weather necessitated our temporary separation. And I expect letters from you every other day confirming your continued wellbeing."

"Of course," she agreed readily, relieved that the matter was settled. "Now, shouldn't you be packing if you're to depart within the hour?"

Chapter 9

As Thomas went to prepare for his journey, Beatrice found herself both excited and apprehensive about the days ahead. With most guests departing and Caroline Blackwood thankfully among them, the reduced company at Thornfield would provide greater freedom for her and James. Yet Caroline's pointed references to the journal remained troubling. Had she actually seen it? Did she know its contents, or was she merely fishing for information based on suspicion?

These questions occupied Beatrice's mind as she helped Thomas prepare for departure, checking that he had everything necessary for the journey back to London. By mid-morning, the entrance hall of Thornfield Estate was crowded with departing guests, servants loading trunks onto carriages despite the continuing downpour.

Caroline Blackwood stood amid the chaos, issuing instructions to her maid with imperious gestures. When she caught sight of Beatrice observing the departures, she broke away from her preparations to approach with a predatory smile.

"How fortunate that you're able to extend your stay, Lady Beatrice," she said, her voice pitched low enough that others wouldn't overhear. "Such a dedicated scholar, seeking... knowledge wherever it may be found."

"The weather makes travel inadvisable," Beatrice replied evenly. "Nothing more complicated than that."

Caroline's laugh held no humor. "Of course. And I'm certain Lord Ashworth's similar decision is equally practical." She leaned closer, her voice dropping further. "A word of advice, my dear—men like James consider innocence amusing until it becomes tiresome. When the novelty of your wide-eyed fascination wears thin, he'll return to women who understand what men truly want without needing... instruction."

The barb was precisely targeted to exploit Beatrice's deepest insecurity—that her inexperience would ultimately prove insufficient to hold James's interest. Yet something in Caroline's spiteful certainty had the opposite effect, strengthening rather than undermining Beatrice's confidence.

"How interesting that you assume to know what Lord Ashworth truly wants," she replied calmly. "Perhaps your understanding is not as complete as you believe."

Caroline's perfect features hardened momentarily before she regained her composure. "We shall see, won't we? Though I doubt you'll enjoy the lesson when it comes." With a final pointed smile, she swept away to rejoin her departing party.

Thomas's farewell was more emotional than Beatrice had anticipated. His obvious concern touched her even as she assured him repeatedly of her safety under Mrs. Thornfield's care.

"Remember your promise," he said, embracing her one last time before climbing into the carriage. "Guard yourself carefully."

"I will," she replied, the words feeling like both truth and falsehood simultaneously. She would indeed guard what mattered—her heart and her autonomy—though perhaps not in the way Thomas intended.

As the carriages pulled away, disappearing into the rain-soaked drive, Beatrice felt a curious mixture of relief and trepidation. For the first time in her adult life, she stood without family to guide or constrain her choices. The freedom was both exhilarating and terrifying.

"They're safely away, then," came James's voice from behind her.

She turned to find him standing in the entrance hall doorway, watching her with an expression that made her heart quicken. Now that most guests had departed, he seemed to have relaxed his careful public mask, allowing his genuine feelings to show more openly.

"Yes," she replied simply, conscious of the servants still moving around them. "My brother extracted numerous promises regarding my safety and reputation before consenting to leave me behind."

A smile touched James's lips. "As he should. Though I wonder what Captain Harrington would think of the specific threats to both that remain at Thornfield."

The playful comment held a serious undertone that Beatrice couldn't ignore. "Caroline made a point of speaking to me before she left," she said, lowering her voice. "She knows about the journal, James. Or at least suspects enough to be dangerous."

His expression turned more serious. "I feared as much from her comments in the library. The question is whether she has actual knowledge or merely suspicion."

"And whether she's likely to act on either," Beatrice added.

Before he could respond, Mrs. Thornfield approached them, her expression warmly conspiratorial. "My dears, now that our more conventional guests have departed, perhaps you'd join me in the small parlor for tea? There are matters I think we should discuss with fewer ears present."

The invitation surprised Beatrice, though James seemed to have expected it. He offered his arm to their hostess with easy familiarity. "Lead the way, Eleanor. I suspect this conversation is overdue."

Curious and slightly apprehensive, Beatrice followed them through the now-quiet house to a cozy parlor she hadn't visited before. Unlike the formal drawing rooms used for the house party, this space felt personal—filled with comfortable furniture, well-used books, and mementos that suggested private history rather than public display.

Mrs. Thornfield settled into a wingback chair near the fire, gesturing for them to take the small sofa opposite. Once a maid had brought tea and been dismissed with instructions not to disturb them, their hostess regarded them with clear-eyed directness.

"I think it's time we spoke plainly," she began, pouring tea with practiced elegance. "Your interest in each other has been obvious to me since the second day of the house party, though you've both made admirable efforts at discretion."

Beatrice felt heat rise to her cheeks, but James merely smiled ruefully. "We should have known we couldn't fool you, Eleanor."

"Indeed not," the older woman agreed with a smile. "I've known you since boyhood, James, and I recognize the signs of genuine attraction versus your usual careful distance. And Lady Beatrice—you have an expressive face that betrays your feelings even when your words and actions remain proper."

Unsure how to respond to such direct acknowledgment of what had been carefully concealed, Beatrice accepted her teacup in silence.

"I want you both to know," Mrs. Thornfield continued, "that while society would condemn your obvious connection, I do not. In fact, I've done what I could to facilitate it—from arranging riding parties to creating diversions at the masquerade."

James reached for Beatrice's hand, squeezing it gently. "We suspected as much, though your motives remained unclear."

Mrs. Thornfield's expression softened. "My motives are

simple: I believe in love, genuine love, wherever it may be found. Society's rules too often prevent such connections in favor of suitable matches based on wealth, title, or family alliance."

She set down her teacup, her gaze turning more distant. "As James may have told you, Lady Beatrice, I had my own great love many years ago. Edward Cavendish—a younger son with no fortune or prospects, considered entirely unsuitable for the daughter of an earl. We were forced to conduct our affair in secret, stealing moments at house parties not unlike this one, communicating through letters and private signals."

"James mentioned he died before you could marry," Beatrice said softly.

Mrs. Thornfield nodded, pain briefly visible in her eyes despite the decades that had passed. "Fever took him three weeks before we planned to elope. I received news of his death on the very day I had planned to leave a note for my parents explaining our intentions."

"I'm so sorry," Beatrice said, moved by the older woman's lingering grief.

"It was long ago," Mrs. Thornfield replied with a sad smile. "But the experience taught me that life is too short to sacrifice genuine happiness for social convention. When I see two people who have found that rare connection, I cannot in good conscience stand in their way—even if society would expect me to do precisely that as your hostess and temporary guardian."

James leaned forward slightly. "What exactly are you saying, Eleanor?"

"I'm saying," she replied directly, "that while you remain at Thornfield, I will neither monitor nor restrict your private interactions. My staff is both loyal and discreet. What occurs under my roof stays under my roof."

The implication was unmistakable. Mrs. Thornfield was effectively removing all barriers to Beatrice and James pursuing their relationship however they chose, without fear of discovery or social consequences.

"That's... extraordinarily generous," Beatrice managed, stunned by the freedom being offered.

"It comes with one condition," Mrs. Thornfield added, her expression turning more serious. "Complete honesty with each other about intentions and feelings. I will not facilitate a dalliance that leaves either party wounded or used. So I must ask directly: What do you seek from this connection?"

The blunt question hung in the air between them. Beatrice looked at James, uncertain who should speak first or what could be said that wouldn't sound either presumptuous or inadequate.

James met her gaze briefly before turning to Mrs. Thornfield. "I love her," he said simply. "Not as a novelty or a conquest, but as the woman who saw beyond my reputation to the person beneath. My intention, should Beatrice be willing, is marriage."

The declaration, spoken so directly, stole Beatrice's breath completely. Though their connection had grown increasingly profound, neither had put such definitive words to their feelings or intentions.

Mrs. Thornfield nodded, apparently unsurprised, and turned her attention to Beatrice. "And you, my dear? What do you seek from James?"

Put on the spot, Beatrice found herself momentarily speechless. The proper response would be demure uncertainty or coy deflection. Instead, she found herself answering with the same directness James had shown.

"I love him as well," she said, the words feeling both terrifying and liberating as they left her lips. "Not the Earl of

Westmoreland that society sees, but the man who writes his deepest thoughts in a hidden journal and values my mind as much as my body. As for marriage..." She hesitated, then continued honestly, "I hadn't allowed myself to consider it as a real possibility until this moment."

James's hand tightened around hers, his expression a mixture of joy and vulnerability that made her heart ache. "It is very real, Beatrice. The most real thing I've ever offered anyone."

Mrs. Thornfield smiled, satisfaction evident in her expression. "Then my condition is met. What happens next is entirely your choice, with my blessing and protection for as long as you remain at Thornfield."

She rose, signaling the end of their unusual conversation. "I believe I'll rest in my chambers this afternoon. The excitement of managing departures has quite tired me. I likely won't emerge until dinner at eight." The pointed information about her whereabouts was unmistakable in its intention.

As their hostess left them alone in the parlor, Beatrice found herself overwhelmed by the sudden removal of all constraints. The freedom to act on their feelings without fear of discovery or judgment was both thrilling and intimidating.

"Did you mean it?" she asked quietly once the door had closed behind Mrs. Thornfield. "About marriage?"

James turned to face her fully on the sofa, taking both her hands in his. "With all my heart," he replied. "Though I had planned a more romantic proposal than being interrogated by Eleanor Thornfield over tea."

A smile tugged at Beatrice's lips despite her racing heart. "It was rather direct."

"She's always been so," he said fondly. "It's partly why I trust her completely." His expression grew more serious. "But the question remains: what do you want, Beatrice? You said you love me, which makes me happier than I can express, but marriage is a significant step—one that would bind you to a man whose reputation might cause you social difficulties."

The concern in his voice touched her deeply. Even now, with his own desires clear, he was prioritizing her wellbeing and happiness.

"Your reputation concerns me far less than it once did," she said honestly. "The man I've come to know through your journal and our time together bears little resemblance to society's portrayal of you. And even if some of that reputation was deserved in the past, people change. I believe in who you are now."

Relief and gratitude washed over his features. "Then will you consider my suit? Not because Eleanor prompted it or because we've shared intimate moments, but because you might envision a life with me as your husband?"

The formal phrasing contrasted with their decidedly unconventional courtship, making Beatrice smile even as tears pricked at her eyes. "I do envision it," she admitted. "Though I fear I'd make a terrible countess. I'm too bookish, too opinionated, and apparently too willing to break social conventions."

James laughed, the sound warming her from within. "You would make a magnificent countess precisely because of those qualities. My estate needs someone who thinks beyond tradition, who values substance over appearance. And I need a partner who challenges and understands me, not an ornament who merely decorates my arm at social functions."

His hands released hers to cup her face gently. "Marry me, Beatrice Harrington. Be my wife, my lover, my intellectual equal, my heart's companion. Let me love you openly as I've already begun to love you in secret."

The sincerity in his voice and eyes undid her completely. "Yes," she whispered, tears spilling onto her cheeks. "Yes, I'll marry you, James."

His kiss was gentle at first—a seal on their commitment—but quickly deepened into something more urgent as the reality of their new understanding took hold. His arms encircled her waist, drawing her closer on the sofa as her hands found their way into his hair.

When they finally broke apart, both breathless, James rested his forehead against hers. "We should write to your father immediately," he said. "And to your brother. I want to do this properly, with their blessing if possible."

The consideration touched her, though she couldn't help laughing softly. "My father will be shocked. He had nearly resigned himself to my spinsterhood after three unsuccessful seasons."

"Then he'll be pleasantly surprised," James replied with a smile. "Though perhaps we should omit the more... unconventional aspects of our courtship from the official narrative."

"You mean not mention that I first fell in love with you through reading your explicit journal?" Beatrice teased. "How disappointing. It's such a romantic beginning."

His laugh was rich with genuine amusement. "Perhaps we'll save that version for our grandchildren."

The casual reference to their future family sent a wave of warmth through Beatrice. For the first time, she allowed herself to fully imagine a life with James—not just the immediate pleasure of his company, but the years stretching ahead as husband and wife, perhaps parents, growing old together with both intellectual and physical connection.

"I should write those letters now," James said reluctantly, clearly not wanting to leave her side. "The sooner we have your family's blessing, the sooner we can announce our engagement formally."

"And in the meantime?" Beatrice asked, suddenly shy despite everything they had already shared.

His eyes darkened with unmistakable desire. "In the meantime, we have Eleanor's blessing within these walls. And several hours before dinner."

The implication sent heat rushing through Beatrice's body. "Where shall we go?" she asked, her voice barely above a whisper.

"My chambers are in the east wing," he replied, his thumb tracing her lower lip in that way that never failed to make her pulse quicken. "Far from the remaining guests and staff quarters. We would have complete privacy."

The suggestion was scandalous even with Mrs. Thornfield's tacit approval. To visit a gentleman's bedchamber, to potentially consummate their relationship before marriage—these were boundaries Beatrice had never imagined crossing before meeting James.

Yet as she looked into his eyes, she found no hesitation within herself—only certainty that this man, this connection, was worth whatever social rules might be broken in its pursuit.

"Show me," she said simply, rising from the sofa and offering her hand.

Chapter 10

The journey through Thornfield Estate to the east wing passed in a blur of anticipation. The rain continued to lash against the windows, creating a cocoon of privacy as they moved through corridors where few servants ventured during afternoon hours. James led her with confidence, his hand warm around hers, occasionally stopping to steal kisses in secluded alcoves.

Finally, they reached a heavy oak door at the end of a quiet hallway. James produced a key, unlocking it with a steady hand that belied the desire evident in his eyes.

"Last chance to reconsider," he said softly as the door swung open. "I would wait forever if you asked it of me."

Beatrice's answer was to step past him into the room, her decision made with both heart and mind in rare agreement.

James's chambers were exactly as she might have imagined—masculine but tasteful, dominated by a large four-poster bed with dark blue hangings. A fire burned in the grate despite the afternoon hour, casting golden light across polished wooden surfaces. Books and papers suggested he actually used the space for reading and correspondence rather than merely sleeping.

The click of the door closing behind her made Beatrice's heart leap into her throat. They were truly alone now, with no possibility of interruption and no need for restraint.

James moved to stand before her, his expression a mixture of desire and tenderness that made her breath catch. "We can go slowly," he assured her, his hands coming to rest lightly on her waist. "Or simply talk, if you prefer. There's no requirement to do anything you're not entirely certain about."

The consideration in his words moved her deeply. Even now, with desire evident in every line of his body, he was putting her comfort above his own needs.

"I am certain," she said, finding courage in his restraint. "About you. About us. About this moment." Her hands rose to the buttons of his waistcoat, beginning to unfasten them with newfound boldness. "Show me everything, James. Make me yours completely."

His sharp intake of breath was the only warning before his control seemed to break. His mouth claimed hers in a kiss that contained all the passion they had been restraining in public—hungry, demanding, yet still attentive to her responses. His hands moved more freely now, exploring the curves of her body through her dress, tracing the line of her spine down to the swell of her hips.

Beatrice responded with equal fervor, her fingers continuing their work on his waistcoat until it hung open. Next came his cravat, which she untied with growing confidence, revealing the strong column of his throat. When her hands moved to the buttons of his shirt, however, he caught them gently.

"Let me undress you first," he murmured against her lips. "I've dreamt of it since the conservatory."

She nodded, turning to allow him access to the buttons that ran down the back of her lavender day dress. His fingers were deft, each button coming undone with practiced ease. As the bodice loosened, he pressed kisses to each new inch of skin revealed along her nape and shoulders, sending shivers of pleasure down her spine.

When the dress was fully unfastened, he helped her step out of it, leaving her in her undergarments—chemise, corset, and drawers. Unlike their encounter in the conservatory, however, there was no need to stop at this stage of undress.

"You're beautiful," James breathed, his gaze traveling over her form with evident appreciation. "May I?"

At her nod, his hands moved to the laces of her corset, slowly loosening the restrictive garment until she could take a full breath for what felt like the first time that day. As the corset fell away, her breasts strained against the thin fabric of her chemise, the nipples visibly hardened with arousal.

James groaned at the sight, his hands coming up to cup her through the fabric. "I've thought of these since I first touched them," he admitted, his thumbs circling the sensitive peaks. "Perfect."

The praise sent heat flooding through Beatrice, emboldening her further. She reached for the hem of her chemise and pulled it over her head in one fluid movement, standing before him bare from the waist up.

His sharp intake of breath was deeply satisfying. "Beatrice," he whispered, reverence clear in his voice. His hands returned to her breasts, this time with no fabric barrier, cupping their weight and teasing the nipples until she moaned softly.

"Your turn," she said when she could speak again, her hands returning to the buttons of his shirt.

This time he didn't stop her, allowing her to push both waistcoat and shirt from his shoulders, revealing his torso to her gaze for the first time. He was magnificent—broad shoulders tapering to a narrow waist, chest covered with dark hair that arrowed downward past the waistband of his breeches. Muscles shifted beneath his skin as he moved, testifying to regular physical activity rather than the indolent lifestyle many nobles preferred.

"May I touch you?" she asked, suddenly shy despite their state of undress.

His smile was tender as he took her hand and placed it on his chest. "You may touch me anywhere you wish, Beatrice. I am yours as completely as you are mine."

The permission unleashed her curiosity. She explored his torso with gentle fingers, learning the texture of his skin, the firmness of muscle beneath, the way his breath quickened when she discovered particularly sensitive spots.

When her hands drifted lower, hovering at the waistband of his breeches, James groaned softly. "If you continue in that direction, this will end far sooner than either of us might wish," he warned, his voice rough with desire.

Understanding his meaning, Beatrice withdrew her hands, though not without a blush at the clear evidence of his arousal straining against the fabric. "What now?" she asked, conscious of her inexperience despite their previous encounters.

In answer, James swept her into his arms and carried her to the bed, laying her gently on the dark blue coverlet. "Now," he said, his eyes dark with desire as he gazed down at her, "I make good on every promise in that journal. If you'll allow me."

"Please," she whispered, reaching for him.

He joined her on the bed, stretching out beside her to claim another kiss. This one was slower, deeper, his tongue exploring her mouth with leisurely thoroughness as his hands resumed their exploration of her body. From her breasts he moved downward, tracing the curve of her waist, the slight roundness of her stomach, before reaching the waistband of her drawers.

"May I remove these?" he asked, his fingers slipping just beneath the edge of the fabric.

At her nod, he slowly drew the garment down her legs, leaving her completely nude before him. Unlike in the conservatory, where darkness and positioning had preserved some modesty, she was now fully exposed to his gaze in the firelit room.

For a moment, insecurity threatened to overwhelm her. Would her body please him? Would she know how to respond properly? What if—

"You're thinking too much," James murmured, correctly interpreting her expression. "There's no right or wrong here, Beatrice. Only pleasure and connection."

His hand moved to her inner thigh, gently encouraging her legs to part. When she complied, his fingers found her center, already slick with arousal from their kisses and caresses.

"Perfect," he breathed, beginning to stroke her with the same skill he had demonstrated in the library and conservatory. "So responsive, so beautiful."

Beatrice gasped as pleasure built quickly under his experienced touch. Her hips began to move of their own accord, seeking more pressure, more friction.

"That's it," he encouraged, his voice a rough caress. "Show me what feels good."

Emboldened by his words, she reached down to guide his hand, showing him exactly where and how she needed to be touched. The intimacy of the action—directing her own pleasure—was as arousing as the physical sensation itself.

As she approached the now-familiar peak, however, James withdrew his hand. Before she could protest, he moved down the bed, positioning himself between her thighs as he had in the conservatory.

"I want to taste you again," he said, his breath warm against her most intimate place. "May I?"

"Yes," she managed, anticipation replacing disappointment at the interruption.

The first touch of his tongue made her cry out, her hands flying to tangle in his dark hair. He groaned against her, the vibration adding to the exquisite sensation as he explored her with devastating precision.

This time, when pleasure crested, Beatrice didn't try to muffle her cries. She called his name as waves of ecstasy washed through her, her body arching off the bed as James continued his attentions until the last tremor subsided.

As she lay boneless with satisfaction, he moved back up to lie beside her, pressing kisses to her flushed face. "Beautiful," he murmured. "I could watch you find pleasure for hours and never tire of it."

Despite her lingering lassitude, Beatrice was acutely aware that James remained unsatisfied. The evidence of his arousal pressed against her hip through his breeches, impossible to ignore.

With newfound boldness, she reached down to cup him through the fabric. "Show me how to please you," she said softly. "I want to learn."

A groan escaped him at her touch. "Are you certain?"

"Completely," she assured him. "I want all of you, James. Not just parts."

Chapter 10

The honesty in her voice seemed to break the last of his restraint. He rose from the bed long enough to remove his remaining clothing, revealing himself fully to her gaze for the first time.

Beatrice couldn't help staring. She had no basis for comparison, but James appeared impressively endowed, his arousal standing proud from a nest of dark hair. Rather than fear, she felt curiosity and anticipation as he rejoined her on the bed.

"Touch me," he invited, guiding her hand to his length.

The sensation was unlike anything she had experienced—silken skin over hardness, warm and alive beneath her fingers. James showed her how to stroke him, his breathing growing more ragged as she gained confidence in her movements.

"Like this?" she asked, watching his face for signs of pleasure.

"God, yes," he groaned, his head falling back as she continued her exploration. "But if you continue much longer, I won't last."

Understanding his meaning, Beatrice slowed her movements. "What happens now?" she asked, both nervous and eager for what would follow.

James's expression turned serious despite his evident arousal. "Now we decide whether to complete this joining," he said. "If we do, you would no longer be a virgin when we marry. Some men consider that important."

"Do you?" she asked directly.

"Not in the slightest," he replied without hesitation. "But I don't want you to have regrets, either about the act itself or its timing."

The consideration in his words, even at this most intimate moment, confirmed everything Beatrice had come to believe about his character. This was not a man who viewed women as conquests to be claimed and discarded, but as equal partners in pleasure and life.

"My only regret would be stopping now," she said honestly. "I want to be yours completely, James. In every way."

Relief and desire mingled in his expression as he moved above her, positioning himself between her thighs. "This may hurt at first," he warned, the head of his arousal pressing against her entrance. "Tell me if you need me to stop."

Beatrice nodded, her hands coming to rest on his shoulders as he began to push forward. The sensation was strange—a stretching pressure that bordered on discomfort but didn't quite cross into pain. She focused on James's face, on the love and desire evident in his expression as he restrained himself to enter her slowly.

When he encountered the barrier of her maidenhead, he paused, his breathing labored with the effort of control. "Ready?" he asked softly.

At her nod, he pushed forward with one smooth thrust, breaking through the thin membrane that had marked her virginity. A sharp pain made her gasp, her nails digging into his shoulders involuntarily.

James immediately stilled, fully seated within her but not moving. "Breathe," he murmured, pressing kisses to her face, her neck, her lips. "The pain will pass, I promise."

True to his word, the discomfort began to fade, replaced by a curious fullness that wasn't unpleasant. When Beatrice shifted experimentally beneath him, a different sensation sparked—a hint of the pleasure his fingers and mouth had previously provided.

"Better?" James asked, watching her face carefully.

"Yes," she replied, lifting her hips slightly to take him deeper. "You can move now."

With a groan of relief, he began to withdraw and thrust back in with careful control, establishing a gentle rhythm that allowed her body to adjust to the unfamiliar intrusion. Gradually, as discomfort gave way to increasing pleasure, Beatrice found herself meeting his movements, her legs wrapping around his waist to draw him deeper.

"James," she gasped as he hit a spot inside her that sent sparks of pleasure radiating outward. "There—please—"

Understanding her incoherent plea, he angled his hips to strike the same spot with each thrust. His hand slipped between their bodies to find the sensitive bud at the apex of her sex, circling it in time with his movements.

The dual stimulation quickly rebuilt the pleasure that had briefly receded with the initial pain. Beatrice felt herself climbing toward another peak, this one somehow deeper, more profound for the connection they now shared.

"That's it," James encouraged, his voice strained with the effort of maintaining control. "Let go, Beatrice. Come for me again."

The combination of his words, his touch, and the increasingly perfect rhythm of his thrusts pushed her over the edge. She cried out his name as pleasure crashed through her in waves, her inner muscles clenching around him as she shuddered with release.

The sensation of her climax triggered James's own. With a hoarse cry, he pulled out of her body at the last moment, his seed spilling onto her stomach in hot pulses as he found his release.

The consideration of the act—ensuring she wouldn't face pregnancy before marriage—moved Beatrice deeply even in her pleasure-dazed state. When James collapsed beside her, breathing heavily, she turned to kiss him with all the love and gratitude she felt.

"Thank you," she whispered against his lips.

He smiled, brushing damp hair from her forehead with gentle fingers. "For what? That should be my line, I think."

"For making it beautiful," she replied simply. "For caring about my pleasure as much as your own. For loving me enough to show restraint even at the end."

Understanding dawned in his eyes. "Ah. That was practical rather than noble, I'm afraid. While I would happily marry you tomorrow and welcome any child conceived between us, I thought you might prefer a proper wedding without whispers about hasty arrangements."

The practicality made her laugh softly. "Very considerate nonetheless."

James reached for his discarded shirt, using it to gently clean her stomach before pulling her into his arms. They lay together in comfortable silence, listening to the rain against the windows and the occasional pop from the fire.

"No regrets?" he asked finally, his voice holding a hint of vulnerability that touched her heart.

Beatrice propped herself up on one elbow to look at him properly. "None," she said firmly. "Except perhaps that we didn't find your journal sooner."

His laugh warmed her from within. "Indeed. Think of all the time we might have saved."

"Though the discovery process has been rather enjoyable," she teased, pressing a kiss to his chest.

"And educational," he added with a smile. "For both of us."

Beatrice's eyebrows rose in surprise. "What could I possibly have taught you?"

His expression turned serious. "That physical connection, no matter how skilled or pleasurable, pales in comparison to joining with someone who knows your mind as well as your body. That vulnerability can be more arousing than practiced seduction. That love transforms pleasure from momentary release to profound connection."

The sincerity in his voice brought tears to her eyes. "I love you," she whispered, the words still new enough to feel both frightening and exhilarating.

"And I love you," he replied, drawing her down for a kiss that held promise of both immediate pleasures and a lifetime of shared passion. "My beautiful, curious reader who found not just my journal, but me."

As afternoon deepened toward evening, they remained entwined in James's bed, alternating between tender conversation and renewed exploration of each other's bodies. By the time they reluctantly rose to dress for dinner, Beatrice felt transformed—not just by the physical aspects of their lovemaking, but by the profound certainty that in James Ashworth, she had found her perfect match in mind, body, and soul.

Whatever challenges awaited them beyond Thornfield's protective walls—her father's reaction, society's potential censure, the adjustments to life as a countess—she would face them with James beside her, their connection forged through written words and intimate touches, stronger for having begun in honesty rather than convention.

Epilogue

Six months later, Lady Beatrice Ashworth, Countess of Westmoreland, sat at her writing desk in the private chambers she shared with her husband at their Derbyshire estate. Spring sunshine streamed through the tall windows, warming the room despite the lingering chill of early April. Outside, the gardens were beginning to awaken from winter dormancy, the first crocuses and snowdrops creating patches of color against the greening landscape.

Marriage had brought changes both expected and surprising. The transition from daughter of a viscount to countess had required adjustments—learning to manage a large household staff, navigating the complex social hierarchies of county society, finding her place as the new mistress of an ancient estate. Yet James had supported her through every challenge, valuing her intelligence and independent spirit rather than attempting to mold her into a conventional aristocratic wife.

Society had raised eyebrows at their somewhat hasty courtship, of course. Their engagement had been announced immediately upon returning to London, with the wedding following just two months later—quick enough to cause speculation but not so rapid as to suggest absolute necessity. Mrs. Thornfield had been instrumental in quieting the worst of the gossip, her impeccable reputation lending respectability to the match even as knowing looks were exchanged behind fans at society gatherings.

Thomas had been initially skeptical but ultimately won over by the obvious depth of their connection and James's formal request for his blessing. Her father, returning from abroad just in time for the wedding, had been simply pleased that his bookish daughter had secured such an advantageous match, blissfully unaware of the unconventional nature of their courtship.

Caroline Blackwood had made one attempt at scandal, hinting at improprieties during the Thornfield house party, but found herself swiftly ostracized from the best circles when Mrs. Thornfield countered with pointed references to Caroline's own indiscretions. The threat had dissipated quickly, leaving Beatrice and James to build their life together in peace.

Now, as Beatrice put the finishing touches on a letter to her brother, she heard the door to their chambers open. Without turning, she knew it was James—his footsteps, his scent, even the quality of his silence had become as familiar to her as her own heartbeat over the months of their marriage.

"Writing to Thomas again?" he asked, coming to stand behind her chair and placing his hands on her shoulders. "You'll run out of news if you correspond so frequently."

Beatrice tilted her head back to smile up at him. "Never. The estate provides endless material, and I haven't even told him about your plans for the new library wing."

James bent to kiss her upturned face, his lips lingering against hers with the same tenderness that had characterized their first encounters. Six months of marriage had done nothing to diminish their desire for each other—if anything, the freedom to explore without constraint had only deepened their physical connection.

"Speaking of libraries," he said when they parted, "I have something for you."

From behind his back, he produced a leather-bound journal identical to the one that had brought them together at Thornfield Estate. The original now resided in a locked drawer in Beatrice's writing desk, its explicit contents too private to risk even the most discreet servant discovering.

"A new journal?" she asked, accepting the gift with curious hands.

"I thought we might continue our written correspondence, even though we no longer need it for clandestine communication," he explained, a hint of vulnerability in his expression. "There's something powerful about putting thoughts to paper—a different kind of intimacy than what we share in bed or in conversation."

The thoughtfulness of the gift touched her deeply. "I'd like that," she said softly. "Though what shall we write about now that we have no need for secrecy?"

A slow smile spread across James's face as he knelt beside her chair. "Perhaps our hopes for the future? Our reflections on the past? Or simply the thoughts that come to us when we're apart during the day, too private to share with anyone but each other."

His hand came to rest gently on her stomach, which had just begun to show the slightest curve—visible only to those who knew to look for it. "And perhaps someday, it might become a record of this new chapter in our lives. Something to remind us of these early days when our family was just beginning."

Tears pricked at Beatrice's eyes at the tenderness in his voice. They had only confirmed the pregnancy two weeks ago, their joy tempered with the caution that came with first expectations. The fact that James was already thinking of documenting this journey for their future child moved her beyond words.

"I think that's beautiful," she managed, covering his hand with her own. "Though perhaps we'll create a separate volume for those reflections. This one can remain exclusively for husband and wife."

His eyebrows rose in amusement. "Planning to continue our more explicit exchanges, are you?"

"Absolutely," she replied with newfound confidence. The shy, proper Lady Beatrice who had first discovered his journal still existed somewhere within her, but she had been joined by a woman who knew her own desires and wasn't afraid to express them. "Pregnancy doesn't diminish desire, as you've already discovered."

James laughed, the sound rich with happiness and promise. "Indeed it doesn't. Particularly when the mother-to-be grows more beautiful by the day."

He rose, pulling her gently to her feet and into his arms. "Shall we christen the new journal immediately? I find myself with several hours free before dinner, and a wife who inspires the most poetic thoughts."

"Poetic?" she teased, allowing him to guide her toward their bed. "Is that what we're calling those explicit descriptions now?"

"In the right hands, the explicit can be quite poetic," he countered, his fingers already working on the buttons of her day dress with practiced ease. "As you've demonstrated repeatedly in your own contributions."

As clothing gave way to skin, and conversation to more immediate forms of communication, Beatrice reflected on the extraordinary journey that had brought them to this point. A hidden journal, a curious reader, forbidden words exchanged in secret—leading to a love that had transformed both their lives completely.

Later, as they lay entwined in the afternoon sunshine streaming across their bed, James reached for the new journal and quill from her nightstand. With careful consideration, he opened to the first blank page and wrote a single line before passing it to her:

To my wife, whose curiosity opened not just a journal but my carefully guarded heart—I remain eternally grateful for your courage in writing back. - J

Smiling through tears of happiness, Beatrice took the quill and added her response beneath his words:

To my husband, whose hidden depths first captured my mind before claiming my body and soul—thank you for seeing the woman beneath society's constraints and loving all that you found there. Forever yours, - B

As James pulled her close again, the journal slipped forgotten to the floor beside their bed—the first entry of many in what would become another treasured record of their unusual but perfect love story, begun in secret at Thornfield Estate but continuing openly in the life they now shared.

In the years to come, they would fill many such journals—some with thoughts too intimate to share beyond their marriage bed, others with reflections on parenthood, partnership, and the evolving nature of love over decades together. But none would ever quite match the significance of that first discovery: a curious lady, a hidden diary, and the transformative power of words written in ink but felt in the heart.

About the Author

Elena is a passionate writer of historical romance, crafting stories that span everything from brooding Victorian affairs to bawdy, outlandish pirate adventures on the high seas. Whether serious or cheeky, her tales are always rich with atmosphere, irresistible tension, and scenes that turn up the heat. Her books are perfect for readers who love history served with a wink—and a good deal of steam.

When she's not writing, Elena enjoys baking elaborate pastries and wandering antique shops in search of inspiration for her next story. She has a particular fondness for old letters and vintage postcards, often imagining the secret romances they once held. Her love of history and flirtation with the sensual makes its way into everything she creates.

Printed in Dunstable, United Kingdom